CANYON WINTER

Peter jammed his face into the sleeping bag and pushed it against the instrument panel with all his strength. But his whole body was alive to what was happening. He heard snapping, scraping. The plane lurched drunkenly. He guessed they had hit the top of a tree. The plane righted momentarily. Then the cabin was spinning over and over. The safety belt cut into his middle. There was the tortured rending and buckling of metal, a thunderous explosion. The sleeping bag was ripped from his face. Something crashed against his head. Then he was hurtling through space. . . .

OTHER PUFFIN BOOKS YOU MAY ENJOY:

Bones on Black Spruce Mountain   David Budbill
Bristle Face   Zachary Ball
The Call of the Wild   Jack London
Dogsong   Gary Paulsen
Drifting Snow   James Houston
The Falcon Bow   James Houston
Hatchet   Gary Paulsen
Lad: A Dog   Albert Payson Terhune
My Side of the Mountain   Jean Craighead George
Rascal   Sterling North
River Runners   James Houston
White Fang   Jack London
The Wolfling   Sterling North
Woodsong   Gary Paulsen

Canyon Winter

WALT MOREY

PUFFIN BOOKS

To Annette Tussing and all the defenders
of Hell's Canyon, and to Gary Eisler,
protector of our forests

PUFFIN BOOKS
Published by the Penguin Group
Penguin Books USA Inc., 375 Hudson Street, New York, New York 10014, U.S.A.
Penguin Books Ltd, 27 Wrights Lane, London W8 5TZ, England
Penguin Books Australia Ltd, Ringwood, Victoria, Australia
Penguin Books Canada Ltd, 10 Alcorn Avenue, Toronto, Ontario, Canada M4V 3B2
Penguin Books (N.Z.) Ltd, 182–190 Wairau Road, Auckland 10, New Zealand

Penguin Books Ltd, Registered Offices: Harmondsworth, Middlesex, England

First published in the United States of America by E.P. Dutton, 1972
Published in Puffin Books, 1994

1 3 5 7 9 10 8 6 4 2

Author's Note

Canyon Winter is fiction. This statement is made because persons who know the Seven Devils Country and the canyons of the mighty Snake River will realize the writer has taken certain liberties with the topography of the region. There is no Omar's Wilderness and cabin or Flat Iron Creek. But in this primitive area there could be.

The descriptions of the Snake River and Hell's Canyon are true, as are mention of certain destructive logging practices and the fight that is evolving over them.

The plane had crashed in the primitive fringe of the Rockies known as the Seven Devils. It is almost inaccessible to man. It is a vast region of virgin forests, towering mountains, and deep, sheer-walled canyons through which plunge foaming rivers. Here the eagle soars, the mountain lion stalks his prey, salmon and trout flash in crystal streams of a primeval forest that was old when Columbus discovered America.

The only travel must be on foot or horseback over tortuous mountain trails, and only in spring and summer during the snow thaw. When the runoff raises the river level, powerful jet boats battle their way into this mountain fastness to give a few hardy tourists the heart-stopping thrill of riding white water.

A few tough old prospectors and trappers who have turned their backs on civilization eke out an existence here. There is peace and solitude and an unhurried way of life. Coyote, bobcat, cougar, deer, elk, goat, bear, and a host of small animals abound. Salmon battle their way up from the sea to spawn in the feeder streams, and many migratory waterfowl nest and raise their young.

The plane had flown over this country in late fall when peaks and ridges were blanketed deep with snow.

Peter Grayson, the passenger, looked down through the side window from four thousand feet. He was neither concerned nor interested. Frank Eldridge was a good pilot. He flew exclusively for Grayson Electronics. Peter had flown with him before, usually with his father along. This time they were to meet at the ranch high in the Cascades. It wasn't really a ranch. A half-dozen wealthy men and his father had fenced off a couple thousand acres of rough country. They imported wild animals into the enclosure and hunted them.

Peter didn't think much of it as sport, and he'd have liked to say "No." But no one argued with George Grayson.

The boy knew his father was disappointed in him. He'd never have his father's big, bruising frame. His bones were long enough, but he was lightly muscled even for fifteen. He tended to be slender, like his mother.

He'd overheard his father talking about him. "Kid's not even interested in any kind of sport. It's not normal for a boy—a boy of mine anyway."

"He's doing very well in school," Clara Grayson smiled.

"You know what I mean. Someday he'll head up

2

Grayson Electronics, or he should. That tak
man, a fighter. He doesn't seem to have an
qualities."

"Give him time, George."

"All the time in the world won't help him. He's not
doing a thing to develop any kind of toughness."

"What do you expect of a fifteen-year-old?"

"Some indication of what the man's going to be."

"Maybe you'd like him to become a hunter like
you?"

"We've had some pretty famous ones, Boone,
Crockett, Teddy Roosevelt, a host of champion ath-
letes and big-business men. Hunting'll bring out the
man in a boy if it's there. Felt ten feet tall when I
bagged my first deer."

His father was silent a moment. "Not a bad idea,"
he said finally. "Not bad at all."

A few nights later George Grayson had given Peter
the rifle.

Now Peter was flying to the ranch to join his father
in a week-long elk hunt, but he'd rather be back in
school. This would be his first hunt, but his second
time at the ranch. Peter glanced at the pilot. They
hadn't flown over scenery like this the previous time.

Frank Eldridge grinned. "About twenty miles or so
off our flight plan," he explained, "but I want to look
at this country." He pointed down where some of the
most rugged land in North America rolled beneath the
wings. "The finest hunting and fishing left in the

3

United States is right down there. Real virgin land. I wanta bring your dad up here sometime. He'll love this."

Peter nodded. Frank Eldridge lived to hunt and fish and fly.

The nose of the plane tilted down. They sailed into a deep gorge between granite cliffs which confined the brawling course of a river.

"Bet there's eighteen-inch trout down there," Eldridge said, excited. "And goats in those rocks." He brought the plane closer to the sheer rock face. "Maybe we can spot one." They dropped lower into the canyon. Peter could see shark-tooth rocks jutting out of the foaming river channel. They rounded a shoulder of canyon, fled down a long, straight stretch around a sharp bend and Eldridge pointed. "There! Look there! About halfway up. Goats! Two of 'em!"

Stuck to the side of the canyon wall, they looked about as big as rabbits. They began leaping upward from ledge to ledge, fantastically surefooted. The plane passed the goats and fled up a narrow section of gorge, heading for sheer rock walls. Eldridge eased back on the wheel to climb out of the canyon. That moment, the motor sputtered and died. He worked swiftly with knobs, and the motor caught. They began to climb steadily to clear the wall. They were almost over when the motor died again. Eldridge fiddled with the knobs, fingers flying. The motor refused to catch.

Before his eyes Peter saw the propeller slow and stop. Wind whistled past the cabin. They began to lose

4

altitude. The canyon wall rushed at them. Eldridge banked away, working frantically to start the motor. The rock-strewn, tree-studded canyon floor came up fast.

Peter watched Eldridge's intent face and flying fingers. Fear tightened his stomach. "Frank!" His voice sounded high and sharp, "We're going to crash! What'll we do?"

Eldridge didn't take his eyes from their flight course. He had straightened the plane. They were shooting up the canyon in a long glide. "There's a couple of sleeping bags on the floor behind your seat. Wedge one in front of you against your knees and stomach. Hold the other against the instrument panel and press your face into it."

Panic broke through Peter. "We'll be killed!" he screamed. "We'll be killed!"

"Do as I say," Eldridge yelled. "Now!"

In a frenzy Peter unbuckled his seat belt, squirmed around, and dug both sleeping bags from behind the seat. He hurriedly rebuckled the belt and packed one bag against his knees and stomach. He held the second against the instrument panel and watched with horrified fascination. Wind screamed along the wings. The plane seemed to drift sideways, and Eldridge kept fighting it. The rock walls closed in, widened out, closed in again. They left the river for a dry side canyon as the pilot searched for a landing spot. The floor fled beneath the wings, rocks, brush, trees. No clear, flat stretch to set a plane down.

5

Abruptly Eldridge quit trying to start the motor and gripped the wheel with both hands. "When I say 'Now!' shove your head against that sleeping bag as hard as you can and keep it there no matter what happens. Understand?"

"Yes," Peter said.

"Get ready." Eldridge kept watching the floor of the canyon. He shoved the nose down. The tops of the high trees flashed beneath. He pulled the nose up again.

"Now!"

Peter jammed his face into the sleeping bag and pushed it against the instrument panel with all his strength. But his whole body was alive to what was happening. He heard snapping, scraping. The plane lurched drunkenly. He guessed they had hit the top of a tree. The plane righted momentarily. Then the cabin was spinning over and over. The safety belt cut into his middle. There was the tortured rending and buckling of metal, a thunderous explosion. The sleeping bag was ripped from his face. Something crashed against his head. Then he was hurtling through space.

6

🌲🌲🌲🌲🌲🌲🌲 2 🌲🌲🌲🌲🌲🌲🌲

Peter lay flat on his back, and the warmth and solidness of the earth was good. The brightness of the sun was against his closed lids, but he didn't want to open his eyes. He lay there for several minutes afraid to move, trying not to think. Finally he moved one arm, then the other. He did the same with his legs. Nothing seemed to be broken. His head ached with a steady throbbing. There was dampness on his forehead. He raised a hand and felt stickiness. Then he opened his eyes and looked at his fingers. Blood!

He explored the wound with careful fingers. There seemed to be a cut about a half-inch long. It had quit bleeding.

Peter sat up carefully and his eyes sought the plane. It lay about thirty feet away. It had come to rest between two big pine trees which stood about fifteen feet apart. Both wings were sheared off. Peter's side of the cabin was ripped away. The propeller was bent and twisted. The windshield was broken. Peter didn't know if he'd been thrown clear or had staggered this far and collapsed. Through the broken windshield he saw Frank Eldridge bent over the wheel. His head hung forward. He was motionless.

Peter got painfully to his feet. The world swam. His head began to pound. He leaned against a rock until the dizziness passed. Then he walked unsteadily to the plane and made his way through the wreckage to the cabin. "Frank," he said in a frightened whisper, "Frank, oh, Frank!"

Peter made himself crawl into the plane and look closely at the pilot. Then he backed out and stumbled away. He felt sick. His legs began to tremble. He sat on the ground and began to cry. A black-and-white bird sailed noiselessly down and landed on a bush. It studied him with beady eyes. After a minute it flew silently away. A pair of jays followed. One yelled at him as it flitted about in the brush as if his grief annoyed it. Then they left.

His grief finally spent itself. His hands were red where he'd wiped his eyes and smeared the blood on his forehead. It needed washing. He rose and looked about. A hundred feet off, a trickle of water wound among the rocks. He went to it, soaked his handkerchief, and washed his forehead. The water was cold and felt good, but it did not stop the throbbing. When he finished, he stood looking at the sheer canyon walls, the mountains rising tier on tier above them into the blue sky. He thought of how this looked from the plane, a nightmare of towering peaks, deep gorges, razorback ridges.

He was alone in the middle of a wilderness with a dead pilot, a wrecked plane, and surrounded by a forest filled with wild animals. Panic threatened to overwhelm him. Then he remembered his father once said, "People die when they're lost, mostly because they lose their heads. Keep your wits about you, and nine times out of ten you'll survive."

His mind raced ahead to the ranch. His father would wait several hours before ordering a search. Then planes would fly over their flight plan.

But they had deviated from that plan to pass over this country. That meant an all-out search spanning five or six hundred miles. Of course his father would have dozens of planes out. But the chances were very good he'd have to spend the night here.

Peter fought down his fear and began to look about and think and plan. Locating him in this little side canyon would not be easy. With the high peaks ringing the canyon and the deep, narrow walls of the gorge, no plane could safely fly low. The thick limbs of the two pines under which the wreck lay made it almost impossible to spot from the air. The canyon floor was strewn with huge boulders and rock piles, so no plane could land. Brush patches and the scattering of trees made it next to impossible for him to get into the open where a speeding plane could see him. He'd have to build a fire to attract attention.

He chose an open spot about fifty feet from the plane and began dragging up dead limbs, brush, and chunks of rotten stumps and logs. The pile had to be big enough to last all night. He worked hard, and this kept him from thinking. Finally he had a huge pile. He found a pitchy limb and smashed it to kindling over a rock. Peter laid his fire in the center of the cleared space. Now when a plane came, all he had to do was touch a light to the pitch and then begin tossing on wood when it flared into flames.

He remembered Frank Eldridge used a lighter for his cigarettes. Peter didn't want to, but he forced himself to return to the plane and feel about in the pilot's pockets until he found the lighter. He got his sleeping bag and returned to the cleared spot.

The sun passed from sight beyond the canyon rim. Sharp coolness flowed down from the high peaks. Luckily, he had heavy clothing. The shadow of the west wall crept across the canyon floor and climbed the opposite face. Search planes should have been in the air a couple of hours by now. It was highly unlikely one would come at night, but Peter didn't want to miss a bet. He began watching the darkening sky. He became hungry and went to the stream for a drink. It helped temporarily.

He sat beside his fire pile and watched the night advance. The strip of sky grew darker, deeper. The shadows of trees, brush, and rocks stretched across the canyon floor. The stars came out. The canyon turned black and mysterious.

Peter had never spent a night in the wild alone. The silence frightened him. It was shattered by a piercing scream from the sky. A great bird sailed majestically over the canyon rim and disappeared. Somewhere an animal yap-yapped. It was followed by a series of long soulful howls. Sound filled the night. It jumped from canyon wall to wall and died in echoes. In the near trees a voice went *whoo-whoo-ooo.* A second later it was repeated from another direction. Eerie, unreal, it floated softly on the charged silence and sent his heart climbing into his throat. The night seemed bigger, emptier, more mysterious than ever.

He wanted to return to the cabin of the wrecked plane, but he couldn't with Frank Eldridge's body cramped over the wheel. Maybe if he lit the fire—he had plenty of wood to last all night. But every animal in the canyon would know where he was. A bird sailed low over his head and disappeared like a ghost among the trees.

That decided Peter. Wild animals are afraid of fire. He got out the lighter and with trembling fingers struck a flame and thrust it into the pitch splinters. Fire leaped and spread and crackled. He tossed on more wood. The cheery glow chased the shadows, and he felt better. He moved closer for warmth and safety.

The yapping came again but it seemed no nearer. Then he saw a pair of eyes glowing like fire watching him from the near dark. He grabbed a flaming stick and hurled it at the eyes with all his strength. A frightened yell burst from him. "Get out of here! Get!" There was a sound like hoofbeats running away. Silence closed in again.

Peter tossed fresh wood on the fire, and the flames

11

leaped up. He settled down to waiting out the night and intermittently feeding the fire. The eerie calling came again from somewhere in the near trees. He decided it must be an owl. His head finally stopped aching. He caught himself nodding. His eyes closed in spite of himself. Peter decided to crawl into the sleeping bag, not to sleep, only to rest. He was afraid to sleep with these wild animals about. He piled plenty of wood close at hand, crawled into the bag, and zipped it up to his chin. The bag was warm, the fire cheerful.

He tried to stay awake by thinking about his home and parents. His father would have called his mother and told her he was missing. Big, sure, confident George Grayson would reassure her that everything was all right. They'd find Peter in a few hours. Peter believed it, too. But for his father and this crazy hunting mania, he wouldn't be in this mess. His father would enjoy being alone out here. For a minute Peter hated his father; his sureness, his strength, his trophy room with its mounted heads and row of rifles, even his sprawling business empire.

The owl hooted again. The sound drifted through the canyon, seeming to come from everywhere and nowhere. He was very hungry. He hoped when his father came tomorrow he'd have plenty to eat.

When he awoke, the sun was up and the fire out. He crawled from the sleeping bag and stood up. He was stiff and sore from bruises he'd sustained in the crash. He glanced at the wrecked plane and Frank Eldridge bent over the wheel. He pulled his eyes away and searched the cloudless sky. This was the day they'd come for him.

Peter was ravenously hungry. He searched through the near brush for some late berries. There was nothing. Finally he went to the creek, got a drink, and returned to the dead fire. Most of the wood and all the pitch was gone. He spent a couple of hours gathering more wood and pitch and laying another fire. By the time he'd finished, he'd worn off much of the stiffness. He sat down near the pile, lighter ready, and searched the sky for a high speck that meant a plane had come for him.

The sun sailed across the sky, throwing its heat into the canyon. Hunger returned to claw at his stomach. He forced himself to go to the plane and search through the storage space behind the seat in hope someone had left something edible. There was nothing. He remembered his new rifle and looked for it. It would be protection, and with it he could kill some small game and cook it over the fire. He found the rifle wedged partially under the seat. The stock was broken, the telescopic sight smashed. He returned to the stream and filled up with water. It no longer helped.

Peter watched the sky until his eyes watered and his head ached. He listened so hard he heard the soft breeze whispering through the pines. Several times he imagined he heard the distant hum of a plane and started to his feet looking frantically about. A pair of ring-necked pheasants fled across the canyon with shrill cacklings, startling him. Several hundred tiny

13

birds flitted through the near brush, then fled swooping across the canyon like a small gray cloud. A great bird circled high in the sky, and for a heart-stopping moment he thought it was a plane.

The sun passed directly overhead and swung down the sky out of sight behind the western canyon wall. Again the shadows crept over him and the heat of the day was gone. For the first time doubt crept into Peter's mind to gnaw at his confidence. Planes had certainly flown the length of their flight plan several times. Now they would be searching blind. He could die of starvation, waiting to be rescued. For the first time Peter thought of trying to hike out. He might find a house or a trail. But once he left the plane, he'd be on his own.

It came to him then that he'd been on his own since the moment the plane crashed. Hunger would begin to weaken him, and he needed all his strength to hike out. He could wait no longer than tomorrow morning. He hadn't the faintest idea which direction to go, but he wouldn't think about that now.

He went to the creek for another drink. Again he looked for berries or something to eat. He found nothing.

It was another chilly night, but he wasn't so afraid. He built the fire big, pulled his sleeping bag close and crawled in. He stayed awake as long as possible, watching the star-studded sky and listening. He saw and heard nothing that resembled a plane. The silence didn't bother him so much. No eyes watched from the dark. The owl called a few times. Some night bird went over with a sharp, crying voice. He didn't hear the wolf again. Hunger pangs kept gnawing at his stomach. He wanted another drink but was afraid to go to the little stream in the dark. His eyes began to droop and burn in spite of himself. He heaped up the fire, zipped up the bag, and slept.

When Peter awoke, the fire was out and it was full day. He crawled out of the sleeping bag and looked at the sky. It was empty and cloudless. Hunger attacked his stomach like cramps. He had to leave this morning to find food and help. He went to the plane and looked about inside the cabin, trying not to see the figure slumped over the wheel. His suitcase was there with extra clothing, but he couldn't carry it. He took a piece of rope and made straps for the sleeping bag so he could swing it over his shoulders.

He was ready to leave. He looked about, trying to decide which way to go. There were two choices: up or down the canyon. Up the canyon would take him deeper into the mountains, further away from help. He thought of the small stream and remembered he'd heard that if you followed any water downstream, you'd eventually come out at some kind of civilization. The river they'd seen from the plane was here somewhere. They'd left it to fly up this side canyon. Maybe the stream would take him to the river.

Peter hesitated. The broken plane with its dead pilot were the only familiar things in this desolate, empty world. He should bury Frank, but he had nothing to dig with. It seemed he should say something in leaving.

He cleared his throat and said, "Goodbye, Frank. Goodbye." Then he walked quickly off through the brush.

The sun broke over the rim and poured the day's first heat into the canyon. Peter stopped at the little stream, drank his fill, and went on. The canyon began to widen. He heard the roar of rushing water. A few minutes later he stumbled out of the brush onto a gravel bar and stood on the bank of the river.

It was deep and wide. The water charged in white-frothed fury out of a narrow gorge up ahead. The rock wall rose sheer for more than a hundred feet on either side. He looked downriver the way he had to go. The canyon narrowed like the mouth of a funnel, just enough to let the racing water through. He didn't dare tackle that wild water. There was no telling how deep it might be. It could sweep him off his feet, and he'd be drowned. If he started into it and the current got hold of him, there'd be no turning back. He was trapped in this canyon.

Peter was trying to think what to do when a deer stepped out of the brush not thirty feet away. It was a magnificent animal with a great rack of horns. Its head was up and turned, looking at him. There was no fear in its big liquid eyes. It seemed to study the boy. It flapped its fanlike ears at some small insect and shook its horns menacingly. It stamped its feet and snorted delicately. Peter stood frozen. Deer were supposed to be afraid, but this buck wasn't. Buck deer were mean

16

and quarrelsome at certain times of the year. He wondered if this was the time. If it charged, he couldn't get away.

The deer started for the small end of the valley, walking slowly, deliberately, as though it were heading for some special place.

Peter looked at the sheer walls. No deer could climb those to get out. It had got into this canyon somehow; then there must be a way out. If the deer could get out, he could. He began to follow, fearful that any moment it might turn and charge him. The deer was in no hurry, and Peter had the odd feeling that it was suiting its pace to his speed, knowing he was following.

Where the sheer walls pinched in, leaving only room for the river, the deer calmly entered the swift water. It waded to its knees, rounded the great shoulder of the canyon wall, and disappeared.

Peter stopped at the river's edge and studied the racing water. It was crystal clear and so swift it resembled flowing glass. The bottom was round rocks. If one of those turned under his foot and he fell, he'd never regain his foothold. The current would sweep him into deep water and he'd drown.

But there was no other way out, and the deer had made it. He stepped into the icy current and cautiously felt his way over the treacherous bottom. He waded to his knees. The fierce grip of the current threatened to jerk his feet from under him. He stopped uncertainly and glanced back at the safe beach. Then he went on. Water boiled over his knees, but it got no deeper.

17

Finally, he rounded the shoulder of rock, and there was the deer, wading ahead of him in shallower water toward a second bulge of rock. The deer disappeared around it.

A minute later, Peter followed the deer and came out onto a dry beach. He was standing at the head of a small valley whose floor was flat. The sheer gorge walls were gone. The land at the edge of the valley sloped gently upward, flowing out in a wide-spreading fan as far as he could see. It rose in a rolling series of mountains that went up and up to meet the high snow line and disappear over the horizon. The whole valley was blanketed with a stand of pine and fir. The trees were as big as any Peter had ever seen.

The deer was walking off through the trees, and angling away from the river. It seemed to know where it was going. Peter followed.

A few minutes later, the deer entered a small clearing. A log cabin and an out-building squatted in the open. The deer went to the out-building where a door hung open, entered, and lay down.

Peter hurried to the cabin and pounded on the door. He knocked again and again. Then he lifted the latch and pushed the door open. The place was being lived in. The faint aroma of cooking hung in the air. A row of frying pans lined the wall beneath a half-dozen open shelves crammed with food boxes and canned food. A wood stove sat in a corner, the box beside it filled with wood. There were pictures on the walls and curtains at the windows. A stack of well thumbed magazines and papers were piled on a stool. Across the room a partially closed door showed the corner of a bed. The door next to it yawned open and Peter looked directly into a small room that apparently served as a storage room. He could see more shelves loaded with cans and packages of food. The table before him held a sugar bowl and a glass-covered dish.

Peter dropped his sleeping bag on the floor and made for the shelves of food. He took down a can of beans, found a can opener in a drawer, and cut out the top. The drawer yielded a spoon. He sat at the table and began to eat. He lifted the lid of the covered dish and found cold biscuits. He began eating one with the beans. He was so starved he wasn't aware of anything until a shadow fell across the table. He looked up into the chill gray eyes of a tall old man who stood scowling down at him.

The old man's skin beneath a stubble of gray whiskers was firm and as brown as a dead leaf. Wisps of white hair peeked from beneath the brim of a shapeless felt hat. He wore a faded red shirt and heavy pants and shoes. He stood, bony fists on hips, sharp eyes digging into the boy.

Peter stopped eating and said uncertainly, "I—I was lost and I found your place and I—I was hungry. I'll pay for it."

"How long's it been since you ate, boy?" The voice was gruff and unfriendly.

"About two days."

"Then quit gobblin' or you'll get sick. Take small bites, and chew it good. Your stomach's gotta get used to food again." He sounded grouchy and annoyed. "Where'd you come from, boy? How'd you get here? You all alone?"

"We crashed two days ago," Peter said. "This morning I followed a deer, and he led me here. The deer went into the shed."

"Then there was somebody with you?" the old man demanded. "Where is he?"

"Frank Eldridge, the pilot," Peter said. "He was killed. He's still in the plane."

"Crashed? How'd it happen?"

"Frank wanted to look at the country and the river. We were down pretty low, and suddenly the motor quit. Frank couldn't get it started again. We crashed in a little side canyon up the river a ways."

"Lookin' at the country and the river, eh?" The old man's eyes narrowed angrily. "So that Mountain Home Loggin' Company sneaked in by plane this time to look the timber over. And they bring a kid along. It serves you right. I got no sympathy for your kind. I oughta take you out and drown you in the river."

Peter dropped the spoon and shoved back his chair, ready to jump and run. "I don't know what you're talking about," he burst out. "We were just flying over, and Frank was looking at the country for a good place to hunt and fish. I never heard of any Mountain Home Logging Company."

"You and that pilot wasn't lookin' over this stand of timber to log it, to scalp this land bald as a river rock?" the old man demanded.

"No! Frank Eldridge was flying me to meet my father to go hunting. My father's George Grayson. He manufactures electrical things, Grayson Electronics. I'm Peter Grayson."

"Never heard of your pa or his outfit." The old man rubbed his face with a bony hand. The anger seemed

21

to leave him. "Go ahead and eat," he said gruffly.

Peter moved back to the table and picked up the spoon, but he watched the old man fearfully. Finally he ventured, "What's your name, mister?"

"Pickett," the old man grunted. "Omar Pickett." He went into the pantry, returned with a glass of jelly, and put it before Peter. "Straight biscuits ain't so good," he said as if he begrudged even this small kindness. "Especially cold biscuits. I figured to give 'em to Bill."

"I'm sorry if you were saving them for someone else," Peter said.

"Bill won't mind fresh ones. You want water to wash 'em down? It's in that bucket by the stove."

Peter began to eat again, but he was poised to jump and run.

Omar Pickett stood scowling out the open door, hands jammed into his pockets. "Where'd you say this plane crashed?"

"Up the river in a little side canyon. There's a small stream there."

Pickett nodded, "Know the place. About a mile from here. You crash during the day?"

"About noon, I guess."

"I didn't hear the explosion."

"There wasn't any," Peter said. "It tore off the wings and smashed up the cabin and killed Frank."

"You sure he's dead?"

"I'm sure."

The old man was silent a moment. Then, "Did he file a flight plan?"

22

"Yes, but we were about twenty miles off because Frank wanted to look at this country."

"That's great!" Pickett grumbled. He stood there for another minute, then said, "There's more beans and stuff on the shelf if you're still hungry." He went outside and disappeared around a corner of the cabin.

Peter had finished when Pickett returned carrying a pick and shovel. He leaned them against the cabin wall and came in. "If you're through, let's go."

"Where are we going?"

"To bury the pilot."

"Bury him!" Peter's stomach turned over.

"You said he was dead."

"But they're looking for us. My father will have a dozen planes out. One could fly over any minute. They'll want to take Frank back."

Pickett shook his head, "Never did see a lost person that could think straight. Always figure they'll be found right off. If you'd stuck to your flight plan, they'd likely found you before this. You can bet they've flown your course a half-dozen times. By now they're huntin' blind. There's no tellin'. Every hour your chances get slimmer, so let's get goin'. I don't aim to spend all day at this," he said callously.

Peter followed the old man outside, and they went back over the dim trail the deer had brought him. Pickett carried the shovel and pick slung across his wide shoulder. He moved with a long, easy stride that belied the years his white hair and leathery skin indicated.

At the river Pickett splashed into the water and began wading upstream around the shoulder of rock. Peter followed. They had gone about halfway when he slipped, or a rock turned under his foot, and he fell headlong. Icy water closed over him. Current gripped him with giant strength, and he was swirled toward the deep channel. He fought to regain his foothold, but his legs were cut from under him. He tried to shout to the old man, but a wave struck his face and choked him. Panic claimed Peter. He began to flail the water madly. Then a hand clamped on his wrist, and he was hauled upright. Omar Pickett stood waist deep, holding him. He looked as immovable as rock with the current boiling against him.

Pickett held Peter's wrist while they waded upstream and came out on the little sandbar into the mouth of the side canyon. There he let go of Peter and grumbled, "Clumsiest kid I ever saw!" He walked off.

Peter followed coughing, gagging, and spitting water.

Peter stopped at the dead fire. He could go no closer. Omar Pickett dropped the shovel and pick and went to the plane. He crawled inside, looked about, and carefully examined Frank Eldridge. He returned, took up the shovel, and began probing into the dry earth looking for a soft spot. He found one and began to dig, making a hole about four feet by eight. He alternately dug and picked until the hole was about three feet deep. Then he stepped out, wiped sweat from his face, and handed the shovel to Peter.

"You want me to dig?" Peter asked. The thought of digging in Frank Eldridge's grave was revolting.

"He was your friend," Pickett said.

Peter hesitated, then he took the shovel and jumped onto the hole. The shovel point bounced against the hard earth.

Pickett said, "Use the pick."

Peter used the pick as he'd seen the old man do. It was heavy and unwieldy. This was the first time he'd ever used such a tool. He loosened the hard earth, shoveled it out, then used the pick again.

Pickett sat on a rock and watched. He did not offer to help.

Peter had never done manual labor, and his muscles were soft and flabby. His shoulders and arms began to ache. Sweat ran in his eyes and blinded him. Blisters formed in his soft palms.

Finally Pickett said, "You can quit. That's deep enough."

Peter crawled out of the hole and threw down the shovel. He was hot and tired. He wanted a drink.

"All right," Pickett said, "let's get the pilot."

Peter looked at him.

"He's a big man," Pickett pointed out. "I can't carry him alone."

"I can't," Peter cried. "I just can't."

"Look, boy." The old man's voice was rough, his gray eyes unwavering, "Your friend's dead. It's only right and proper he should be buried and not left settin' in that plane with a broken neck. I don't like this

25

job either. But it's got to be done. So let's get at it, and no more holdin' back." He towered over Peter, his manner belligerent.

A small fear ran through the boy. He followed without a word.

It was all the two of them could do to get Frank Eldridge out of the plane. More than once Peter was on the verge of bolting. But the old man's tough voice held him there until they laid the pilot beside the open grave.

Pickett started to search through Frank's pockets.

"You can't do that!" Peter cried.

Pickett removed the wallet, took out cards, receipts, and almost two hundred dollars in cash. "You figure he still needs these?" he demanded. "He's likely got a wife. She can use this money. And these other papers might be important to her. When you go out, you can take 'em with you." He put the wallet in his pocket and continued his search.

He was a cold-blooded, emotionless old man who showed little respect for the dead pilot. The fear of Omar Pickett continued to grow within Peter.

"I guess that's all," Pickett said finally. "Take his feet, boy."

It wasn't as bad as Peter thought it would be. They finally had the job done and the grave mounded with stones. Pickett whittled a cross, bound the pieces together, and stuck it in the ground. He stood tall and lean, white hair blowing in the warm breeze. "You said he liked to fish and hunt. Then he should rest happy here." He turned to Peter, "You got any clothes or things in the plane we oughta take back?"

"I had a rifle, but the stock and sight are broken. My mother put in a suitcase of clothes. There's Frank's sleeping bag, too."

"We'll take 'em. You're gonna need more clothes."

Peter was about to say that clothes didn't matter. He'd be found soon. But Pickett was already striding toward the plane.

Pickett dug out the broken rifle, Peter's big suitcase, and Frank Eldridge's sleeping bag. He tossed the rifle aside. The suitcase was filled with extra shirts, sweaters, trousers, and an extra pair of heavy shoes. Peter was embarrassed. His mother always packed twice as much as he could use.

"This's good," Pickett said. "You're gonna need these extra clothes." He closed the suitcase and tucked it and the sleeping bag under his arm. "You bring the pick and shovel. Let's go."

At the cabin Peter leaned the shovel and pick against the wall.

The deer came from the shed and stood looking at Pickett, flapping its big ears. The old man put down the sleeping bag and suitcase and dug into his pocket. "You lookin' for a chew, Bill?" It was the first time Peter had seen him smile. Pickett drew a plug of chewing tobacco from his pocket, twisted off a small chunk, and held it in his palm. The deer daintily lifted it and ate it. Pickett patted his neck and scratched his head. "That's all, Bill," he said, "no more."

Peter asked, "Is he the Bill you were saving the biscuits for?"

"Of course. Who'd you think?"

"I thought another man. Your partner maybe."

"Bill's better'n any partner. He never quarrels or argues. He takes what I give 'im and is glad to get it." He patted the deer again, picked up the suitcase and sleeping bag, and went inside. He stood looking about. "First off," he said to Peter, "get outa them wet clothes. Then we've got to build you a bunk. It's a good thing you've got this sleepin' bag. I don't have enough blankets for both of us."

"I can put my sleeping bag on the floor," Peter said. "I won't be here more than a couple of days."

"That's a big maybe."

"But they're looking for me."

"They've been lookin' two days accordin' to you. And there hasn't been a plane over this area yet," Pickett pointed out. "They're searchin' several thousand square miles of country lookin' for one small plane. It's like huntin' a needle in a haystack since you flew off your flight plan. You'd better face it. There's less than one chance in a hundred of them findin' you now."

"But there'll be lots of planes out," Peter insisted. "My father will spare no expense."

"Some things you can't buy," Pickett said bluntly. "One is luck. Luck—that a plane might fly over here. Luck—that they'd see a downed plane that's practi-

cally hidden under two pine trees and brush. Luck—
that if it flew over this cabin, they'd somehow know
you were here. Two days have gone. Those hundred-
to-one chances are getting slimmer."

"We can hike out. My father will pay you anything
to take me out. Anything, Mr. Pickett."

Pickett shook his head and walked outside. "Come
out here, boy." He pointed up at the timber-covered
mountains that rose tier on tier into the sky. "We'd
have to cross that range, and it's already winter up
there. There'd be a couple of miles at most of good
hikin'. Then we'd hit the snow line. It's seventy miles to
civilization through snow that'll be from ten to fourteen feet deep. Even if I could make it, I don't have the
clothes for it, and neither do you."

"It's that far to the nearest town?"

"That's right."

"There must be farms along the way that we could
stop at," Peter said, remembering he'd seen an occa-
sional building as Frank and he flew over the country-
side.

"Sure, but they're miles apart, and I've never gone
that direction. I don't know their locations. Just remember, flyin' over at ten or fifteen thousand feet don't
show you how rugged that country is."

Peter looked toward the river. "How far is it that
way?"

"Figured you'd get around to that soon. Sixty-three
miles. You can forget the river, too. It's tough as the

29

mountains this time of year. I don't have a boat. But no boat could live in this river at low water. Too many rocks, rapids, and waterfalls."

"We could hike downriver just like we went up to the plane wreck," Peter pointed out.

"Sixty-three miles!" Pickett shook his head. "Not a chance. There's holes and stretches of river where the bottom drops off sheer a hundred feet deep."

"Then how do you ever get out?"

"Spring and summer. When the big snow pack melts in the mountains, the water rises as much as twenty and sometimes thirty feet. Then big, powerful jet boats come up. I bring in all my supplies during the summer. The jet boats stop when the water gets low in the fall and winter."

"How can I get out of here if—if a plane doesn't come?"

"You can't, until the first jet boat comes about next April."

"That's almost six months!" Peter was aghast. "I can't stay here. My folks will think I'm—I'm dead."

"They'll know you're alive next April."

"There's just got to be a way out!" Peter insisted. "There's just got to be. My father will pay anything you ask if you'll just take me out. Anything!"

"You've said that before," Pickett reminded him. "I wouldn't try to take you out now for all the money you could pile in a wheelbarrow. Get it through your head, boy. There's no way. If there was, you can bet your life I'd take you." The old man's gray eyes were level and unwavering. "Let's get one thing straight between us, boy. I don't like your being here any more than you do. I've lived here alone on to fifty years. If I'd wanted company, I wouldn't have chosen the likes of you. But you are here. And there's nothin' either of us can do about it. The chances of a plane findin' you are as scarce as hen's teeth. We've both got to accept that and make the best of it. We're gonna see an awful lot of each other between now and next spring."

Peter thought of the long winter months trapped in this desolate canyon, hemmed in by towering mountains and an impassable river. Living in this small cabin with a grouchy, cold-blooded old man would be unbearable. Anything could happen.

4

Omar Pickett put the spare sleeping bag and Peter's suitcase under a shelf in the storage room. Frank Eldridge's wallet and papers went into the top drawer of his dresser. "When you leave, take 'em with you," he said.

Then he began preparing lunch. He got a fire going, and in a matter of minutes the savory odor of baking biscuits and frying meat and potatoes filled the room.

In spite of the beans and biscuits Peter had already eaten he was again ravenously hungry. But he had trouble holding a knife and fork. The blisters raised by the shovel and pick stung and burned when he tried to close his hand.

They spent the afternoon building a rough bunk against the wall for Peter's sleeping bag. The old man worked steadily, scowling and silent. He spoke only to give an order. "There's a couple loose boards leanin' against the wall in the shed. Get 'em for me."

"Is the deer in there?" Peter asked.

"Bill? Maybe, I don't know." The old man straightened and scowled at Peter. "For the love of Hannah, boy! Bill won't hurt you. He's a pet, a tame deer. Now get those boards."

The deer was there. He flapped his big ears and looked at Peter with huge liquid eyes. Suddenly he lunged to his feet, shook his antlers menacingly, and started forward. Peter ran out. He went around to the back where there was an open window and crawled through. The deer had gone outside. The boards were leaning against the wall. Peter tossed them through the window and was about to follow. Something shot out of the gloom straight for his face. He ducked, as a bird sailed silently up to the roof and lit on a beam. It sat and stared malevolently down at him.

Peter scrambled out the window. The deer was fifty feet away. It started for him again, shaking its horns. Peter grabbed the boards and ran.

He said to the old man, "That deer tried to hook me with his horns. And there's a bird out there in the shed, an owl of some kind, I guess. It almost flew right in my face. It could have put my eyes out."

"Bill just wants to be friends," Pickett said, "and the owl's Solomon. He was lookin' for a mouse. I catch one most every day for him and give it to him for supper. He must have had bad huntin' last night to come lookin' for it in the middle of the day. He can lift a mouse off your hand, and you'll never feel his talons." He glanced at Peter, "You've never been around animals." It was not a question, but a statement.

"I live in the city," Peter said. "You can't have any

33

kind of animals except maybe a cat or a dog, if you keep it on a leash."

Pickett grunted and picked up one of the boards, "You're scared of your shadow, boy."

They finished the bunk by evening. Supper was biscuits again, made of dough from a crock that sat on the back of the stove. They were amazingly light. They had a can of warmed, sliced meat, potatoes, and a can of peas.

By the time they'd finished supper, it was getting dark. The old man took the two leftover biscuits, went outside, and yelled, "Bill! Come and get it." The deer came from the shed, shook his antlers, and walked up to Pickett. Peter stood in the door and watched him feed the biscuits to the deer. He talked to him in an intimate voice and patted his neck.

"No deer should eat biscuits less'n they're sourdough," Pickett said. Bill twisted his head and shook his horns. He ate daintily from Pickett's hand while the old man rambled on. "Sometimes I'm not sure you know you're a deer. Kindly remember it, will you? We've got company now, and there won't be so many biscuits. You're goin' to have to do a little more scroungin', like other deer. You understand that?" Bill bobbed his head and stamped his feet, waiting for the last bite. Pickett gave it to him, slapped him on the shoulder, and walked around a corner of the cabin. Bill looked after him, then ambled away among the trees.

Pickett came into the cabin several minutes later,

34

carrying a dead mouse. He said, "Got some traps set in a run out in the grass. Catch one most every day. This's Solomon's supper." He took an old leather glove from the shelf, slipped it on his right hand, and went outside.

Pickett stood about fifty feet from the cabin, pursed his lips, and uttered a soft, hollow *whoo-whoo-ooo*. It was the same sound Peter had heard coming from the trees that first night. Pickett whistled again. The sound was eerie. It seemed to come from everywhere and nowhere. An identical answer came from the dark bulk of the shed. Twice more Pickett whistled and was answered. Peter had the odd feeling the two were talking, that they understood each other. A moment later a bird sailed silently from the shed and lit on a dead limb of the big pine tree near the old man.

Pickett whistled again and the owl answered. Pickett said in a soft whispery voice, "You must have had mighty poor huntin' last night, Solomon. How do I know? You scared the boy half outa his wits this afternoon. He ain't like us. He's city born and bred."

Peter clearly heard the clicking sound in the stillness. He learned later it was the owl snapping his beak.

"I got your supper here. Come and get it." Pickett gave the soft call again and held out his right arm with the dead mouse lying in his gloved palm.

Solomon answered from the tree. The next moment he swooped down. He seemed to hesitate at the tips of the old man's gloved fingers. Then the mouse was gone, and Solomon sailed back to the limb.

35

Pickett said softly, "G'night, Solomon. Good hunt-in'."

Soon after, Peter crawled into his sleeping bag. He was dead tired. He'd never worked so hard in his life.

A little later, he saw Pickett take a small calendar from a drawer, cross off the date, and return the calendar. Then he blew out the lamp and went to bed.

Silence settled over the cabin. The blisters in Peter's palms had burst, and his hands were on fire. He waited until he was sure Pickett was asleep. Then he rose quietly, found a basin, and filled it with water from the bucket. He was sitting at the table in the dark, both hands in the cool water, when the old man came from his room and lit the lamp.

Pickett took one of Peter's hands and looked at the palm. He grunted and without a word went to the shelf, scooped a pat of lard from a pail, and smeared it on the boy's palms. "Rub it around," he said. "It'll do more good than all the water in the river." He blew out the light and returned to his room.

Peter spread the lard, and after a few minutes the dry burning began to leave. He returned to bed. But he could not sleep. The silence was oppressive. It was broken by a series of sharp barks that seemed to come from somewhere above the snow line. It came again, riding the stillness. The wolf! Peter snuggled deeper into the sleeping bag. On the heels of that came the odd *whoo-whoo-ooo* of the owl, Solomon. Peter was sure that it came from the pine tree. Something sniffed explosively at the crack under the door. He shot bolt-upright. A yell poured into his throat. It came again. He knew by the sound it had to be some very large animal. Claws raked the door. After a couple of minutes, the sound was gone.

Peter lay down again.

He was listening intently, when with startling suddenness something landed solidly on his chest. A small animal with intense beady eyes stared into his face. Peter surged upright; a frightened cry burst from him. The animal leaped lightly to the floor, scurried to the door, and disappeared beneath it.

Omar Pickett charged into the room and lit the lamp. "What the devil's going on?" he demanded. He stood tall and lean, looking like some forbidding scarecrow in his long underwear.

"Some animal jumped on my chest and was looking right in my face," Peter quavered. "It ran out through that little knothole at the bottom of the door."

"Oh, that was Marty."

"Marty?" Peter asked.

"A tame marten. He comes in every night. I put out some food for 'im. Tonight, with you here and all, I forgot. He was lookin' for his handout of jerky. He's got a hole in a limb of the big pine. You don't have to worry about Marty."

"I heard a wolf howling, too."

"No wolves left in this part of the state. You heard Lonesome, the coyote. He's yellin' for a mate. Sure hope he finds one."

"You got any other queer animals around?"

37

"Plenty of animals." Pickett's lean, craggy face was twisted into a scowl. "No queer ones though."

"Some big animal was sniffing at the door." Peter was determined the old man should show some concern. "I heard it scratching, trying to get in."

"Heard it. Probably a bear. He smelled food."

"A bear!"

"They come nosin' around now and then lookin' for something to eat."

"Aren't you going after him? Aren't you going to shoot him?"

"Why?"

"He's a bear."

"So he oughta be killed?"

"He's dangerous."

"He's a blackie, not a grizzly. Blackies never look for trouble. They hightail it outa the country the minute they smell a man. Look, boy, no bear or anything else is gonna get in here. This's a log cabin. The logs're big and sound. So's that door. No bear can bend the metal bars I put on these windows. Maybe you like settin' up and yellin' your head off half the night at every little noise. But I ain't stayin' here and holdin' your hand. I want some sleep. So simmer down. Nothin's gonna eat you." He blew out the light and started for his room grumbling, "I spend months gettin' Marty tame enough so's he'll come in and eat something, and you have to spoil it. You could've scared him so bad he'll never come back. Don't know if I can put up with six months of you or not."

38

Peter lay in the dark, ears tuned for other strange sounds. The night was quiet save for the faint grumble of the river, the scrape of a branch against a log. He heard Pickett turn on his bed, and later, the steady sound of his heavy breathing. Peter thought of his home high in the hills above the city. From his own spacious bedroom he could look down on a million lights so bright they dimmed the stars. He could pick out streets and watch the buglike flow of traffic. He wondered what his parents were doing. His father would be wrapped up in the search, sending planes out in all directions, giving orders. George Grayson would refuse to accept a single word of doubt that his son still lived.

It was his mother Peter worried about. She was a slender, quiet woman, not too strong and not aggressive. She'd keep her worries and fears to herself. Her world was Peter and his father, their home and the surrounding grounds. His father would be so busy with the search she'd have no one to lean on. Peter was afraid she might go to pieces. He had to get back as quickly as possible for her sake. And for his own good he had to get out of this desolate wilderness before he became as crazy as the old man.

Peter didn't for a second accept Pickett's explanation that there was no way out of here now. Maybe he didn't want anyone to learn the way in for fear others would follow and disturb his solitude. There was no telling what odd ideas a man might get living alone in such a place for almost half a century.

There had to be a way out, and he meant to find it, if a search plane didn't come for him soon.

Lying there in the dark, he began to plan. Pickett would be happy if a plane came for him, so in the morning he'd gather wood and lay another big signal fire. He'd stay close and wait for a couple of days. If a plane didn't come, then he'd begin searching for the way out of here. He had to hurry before winter clamped down in earnest.

He'd have to be careful so Pickett didn't become suspicious. That would mean getting away for hours at a time so he could search the canyon, the river, and the mountain area. To do that he'd have to learn the old man's habits. Once he found the way out, he'd wait his chance, then slip off. He needed a sleeping bag and enough food to last the sixty or seventy miles out. He was still planning when he fell asleep.

Next morning after breakfast Pickett put on his old floppy felt hat and glanced at Peter, "Goin' to the diggin's. You wanta come?"

"The diggings?"

"Got a mine on a little creek about half a mile downriver."

"A gold mine? You get gold out of it?"

"A little."

"I'd like to see it," Peter hedged, "but I want to get some wood for a big signal fire in case a plane comes over. That is, if you don't mind."

Pickett shrugged, "Go ahead, but don't get your

hopes up. Just be sure you build it in the open where it won't catch the other brush."

Peter watched him leave, swinging off with his long, loose-legged stride. Bill, the deer, came from the shed and trotted up to Pickett. He dug the plug of tobacco from his pocket, twisted off a bit, and fed him. He scratched Bill's ears and then went on downriver. Bill wandered up through the trees.

This was a break for Peter. Now he'd have plenty of chance to look for a way out of here.

Before he began gathering wood for his signal fire, he checked the pantry again. The shelves were loaded with canned meats, vegetables, and fruits of all kinds. This was perfect.

In the next two hours Peter gathered a great pile of wood and laid his fire in a cleared spot about a hundred feet from the cabin. He was ready for a plane to come roaring down the canyon or pop out from behind the high mountains. He stayed close all forenoon, waiting, listening, and watching the sky.

Pickett returned at noon, dirty and sweaty. He glanced at Peter's pile of wood and went into the cabin. He spoke only once as he prepared lunch, "You know how to cook anything, boy?"

"No," Peter said.

Pickett grunted. After lunch he went back downriver without a word.

Peter spent the afternoon as he had the morning. Bill returned and looked at him. He shook his antlers

41

and stamped his feet. Peter was ready to sprint for the cabin. But the deer turned into the shed's dark interior.

Pickett returned, and they ate supper. Afterward, the old man went through the same feeding-talking routine with the deer and owl. He shaved some pieces off a chunk of dry, brown meat he called jerky, put it into a small metal tin plate, and then set it inside the door.

Peter crawled into his sleeping bag. It had been a busy but disappointing day. After Pickett went to bed, Peter heard the tin pan rattling. He made out the long, sleek shape of the animal in the dark.

The next morning began like the first. Pickett went to his diggings. Bill came from the shed and wandered through the trees, heading toward the snow line. Peter stayed near his fire pile.

He didn't hear the plane, perhaps because of the eternal grumbling of the river. He just happened to be looking up at the sweep of the mountains when it sailed into view against the sky. It was so high and small that for a moment he mistook it for a soaring eagle. Then he realized it was a plane. He tore out for the fire pile. He had the lighter in his hand ready when he fell on his knees beside the wood. He thumbed it alight and thrust it into the dry grass. The grass fired. The kindling flared. The bone-dry wood caught with a hissing rush, and flames leaped up. Smoke began to billow skyward. Peter searched for the plane. It was almost over him, traveling downriver. He screamed at the top of his lungs, "Down here! Look down here!

Here! Here!" He waved his arms frantically and ran back and forth in the open to attract attention.

The plane passed over, flying very high. It was leaving! Peter dashed through the brush following it. He tripped and sprawled full-length. He was up again. The plane was getting lower! It was going to turn and come back. They'd seen him!

Then he realized that because the plane was going away, it only appeared to be getting lower. He watched through a blur of tears as it flew from sight beyond the distant shoulder of the gorge wall.

Peter returned to the fire and sat on the ground. He was almost physically sick. He felt like he wanted to die.

The fire had sunk to a bed of dying coals when Omar Pickett returned for lunch. He stopped beside the fire, but Peter didn't look up. "So a plane came," he said. "From which direction?"

Peter pointed.

"Comin' over the mountains flying plenty high; ten, fifteen thousand feet, maybe more."

"They could see me," Peter said in a dull voice. "The fire was going good. There was lots of smoke. They didn't come down. They didn't do anything. Just flew right on down the river. They should have known something was wrong. They weren't even looking," he ended bitterly.

"Maybe it wasn't a search plane."

Peter looked up. The thought hadn't occurred to him.

43

"Now and again, maybe once or twice a year, a plane'll come over. But they always fly high because the gorge has some tricky down-drafts. From a couple of miles up they wouldn't tell anythin'. People know I live here. They'd probably think old man Pickett was burnin' some brush. From that height they wouldn't know you wasn't me. A search plane would have been low, and they'd likely been using glasses. They'd have known it wasn't me and give you some kind of signal. So—it wasn't a search plane." Pickett turned toward the cabin. "Come on, we'll eat."

"I'm not hungry," Peter said.

He continued to sit there. Through the open door he heard the old man getting lunch. The first shock of disappointment began to wear off. A plane had flown over. It had not been a search plane. So a search plane could still come.

Pickett came from the cabin and Peter said stubbornly, "I'm going to get another fire ready."

"Sure," Pickett said and continued on downriver.

Peter gathered wood, laid his fire, and settled down to waiting again. He waited the rest of the day. Maybe tomorrow, he told himself.

In the morning a light frost lay over the earth and curled the edges of the leaves. Peter realized then how little time he had before winter set in. He decided to wait one more day. If no plane came, he'd begin searching for the best way out.

The cloudless sky did not hold even an eagle or hawk all day.

The next morning he could hardly wait for the old man to leave before putting his plan into operation. The moment Pickett vanished downriver Peter lit out through the trees, heading uphill toward the snow line. He meant to check that snow depth for himself and see how rugged the country was on top of those ridges.

The slope was gentle at first. Then it became steeper, the brush thicker. The trees were immense. He hadn't gone a half mile when he stepped into a tiny glade and a half-dozen huge animals heaved out of the grass. All but one took off through the trees. This one turned on Peter. It was the first live bull elk he'd ever seen, but he recognized it instantly from the mounted head in his father's trophy room.

The bull was twice as big as Bill. His polished horns, extending more than four feet above his head, looked deadly. Peter froze, too frightened to move. The elk advanced toward him. He closed the distance to halfway before he stopped. He studied the motionless boy a long minute, seeming undecided. Then he turned and walked away slowly in the direction his cows had fled.

Peter moved with great caution after that. He kept picking out trees to climb in an emergency. He startled two more small herds which took off through the brush.

He met a lone bull coming toward him, and he backed hurriedly to a tree. He grasped a low limb, ready to start climbing, but the bull passed without giving him a glance. He saw several deer browsing on

45

brush, and once he thought he recognized Bill. Finally, he reached the snow line.

The first snow was in small thin patches with soggy ground between. The air had a bite. He buttoned his jacket and turned up his collar. He skirted the snow patches and small drifts, keeping to the open ground. His feet became wet and cold. In a few hundred yards the open ground disappeared. He began wading in snow ankle deep. It rose to his shoe tops, then halfway to his knees. The going was not as smooth as it looked from the plane. There were gullies and ridges and drifts that he didn't suspect until he was into them. Twice he fell into holes that had been snowed over. He passed under snow-laden trees whose branches showered him at the slightest touch. His clothing became damp. The cold began to get to him.

Peter struggled ahead until he was up to his knees. The mountains rose ridge on ridge above him. At the rate the depth was increasing, he'd be over his head if he ever did reach the top. Reluctantly, he admitted Pickett was right. There was no way out this direction. He headed back for the cabin.

He saw deer and elk on the return trip, but he was being careful now and had no trouble. Once he saw huge hand-sized paw prints of a bear. It seemed that most animals were staying below the snow line.

Peter arrived at the cabin the same time Pickett came from his diggings for lunch. The old man glanced at the boy's wet clothing and said, "So you found it deep."

"Yes," Peter said.

Pickett glared at him, "You fool kid. You could've run into a cranky bull elk or an old she bear with cubs and got yourself clawed up or killed, or you could've fallen into a snow hole where I'd never find you. You're a babe in the woods. You keep off that mountain from now on unless I'm along. I'm not about to wade miles through that snow lookin' for you or spend days nursin' you if you get hurt or sick. You understand?"

"I wanted to know what it was like."

"Now you know." Pickett stomped into the cabin to begin making lunch.

They ate in silence, and afterward Pickett returned to the diggings.

Peter decided to hike downriver that afternoon. If he could make a few miles, it should give him a good idea whether he could get out that way.

At the start he followed the narrow trail that Pickett took to his diggings. He went carefully so he'd not run into the old man. The trail turned sharply up a small creek that tumbled into the river. Peter waded the creek and continued on.

Within a half mile the valley end and sheer rock walls rose out of the earth again. T ıver plunged into the narrow walled canyon with a roar. Peter hesitated, tempted to turn back, half frightened by the sight and sound of the rushing water. But this was the only way left. Ahead about a hundred yards was a narrow, sandy beach. He decided to try to wade to it. The water was not deep, and the current along shore not too strong.

He made the beach easily. From there he saw another. He waded to it. This was not as bad as it first looked. The water was low, and stretches of narrow beach lay exposed ahead of him as far as he could see. He went forward steadily deeper into the thundering gorge. Where he had to wade, the water remained shallow. Some places the big rocks were packed so tightly along shore he traversed the distance without wetting his feet.

Peter could not become accustomed to the swelling roar of the river. It pounded through the sheer-walled confines, seeming to gather strength as it went. It raced in breath-catching glides, swirled, and sucked in whirlpools. White water smashed against shark-tooth rocks and exploded into spray as if hurled upward by some mighty pressure. He stopped a number of times, tempted to give up, but the sight of another narrow beach reaching deeper into the gorge pulled him on.

Peter became so engrossed with his progress that he lost track of time until the sun slipped behind the canyon wall and shadows reached across the river and chilled him. He glanced up. The shadow was climbing the opposite wall. Pickett would be returning soon. He had to get to the cabin.

He climbed to the top of a high rock and looked deeper into the canyon. He guessed he'd come about two miles. As far as he could see, the river cut straight through the rock with small, intermittent beaches lining either shore. It would be slow, hard traveling. He'd have to be especially careful, but now he knew he could get out this way. A surge of elation lifted his spirits for the first time since the plane crash. Sixty-three miles, Pickett had said. He'd find an inhabited cabin or home long before he traveled that distance.

Peter hurried going back, his mind filled with the next step in his plans. He took a shortcut through the trees to save time. He was nearing the cabin when he came into a small cleared spot and was brought up short by a grave. He hadn't seen it as he gathered wood for his fire because it was hidden behind three huge rocks. The grave was covered with stones just as Frank Eldridge's was. There was a small wooden cross at one end. Not a weed or blade of grass grew on the grave. The surrounding area was cleared and well cared for. Several clumps of recently pulled grass lay nearby.

Peter looked at the grave a minute, then hurried on to the cabin.

Pickett had not returned. He changed his wet clothing, wrung them out, and spread them under his sleeping bag out of sight where they could dry. He'd finished when Pickett walked in.

The old man barely glanced at him. He went to the stove, shook down the ashes, and started a fire. After washing up, he got down frying pans and kettles and began to prepare supper. Bill came to the door and looked in. The spread of his horns almost blocked the opening.

Pickett smiled and shook a fork at him, "Beat it. I'll save you a couple of biscuits." Bill turned and wandered off toward the shed. The old man spoke to Peter only once, "You and Bill don't hit it off very good."

"He doesn't like me," Peter said. "He's always shaking those horns at me."

They ate in silence. Peter finally ventured, "I found a grave out there in a little cleared spot today."

"That so." Pickett went on eating.

"It looks like it's been there a long time," Peter said finally.

"A long time," Pickett agreed.

Peter waited, hoping the old man would volunteer some explanation. At last he asked, "Was it someone you knew?"

"I knew 'im."

"He was a friend of yours?"

Pickett thought a minute then he said, "I'm not sure. Maybe, in a manner of speakin'."

"Oh." Peter waited again. Then he asked, "What did he die of?"

"Didn't. He was killed."

"He had an accident?"

Pickett glanced up, then down at his plate. He took so long Peter thought he wasn't going to answer. Then he said, "It was no accident."

"You mean he was bad? Like a robber or something?"

"There was nothin' bad about him," Pickett said thoughtfully. "He was a fine young man. Very brave."

Again Peter waited. He didn't want to ask the next question, but he'd worked up to it and couldn't stop. "Who killed him?"

Omar Pickett laid down his fork. His gray eyes were almost black. His hawk-sharp face was set. His voice was rougher than Peter had ever heard it, "I killed him, boy. Now, will you shut up?"

Peter sat stunned. He looked into the angry eyes, and his mouth was dry. After a few seconds, Pickett took up his fork and continued eating. Peter tried, but he'd lost his appetite. Oppressive, deadly silence settled between them.

Now Peter knew why the old man had lived here alone in this awful canyon for almost fifty years. Maybe, somehow, this was part of the reason he didn't want Peter to find his way out of here. So this was what a murderer looked like, lean, leaf-brown, and tough. There was no warmth or sympathy in him. He could confess to having killed, then continue calmly to eat. He could rifle the pockets of the dead, as he had Frank Eldridge's, and show no emotion.

The fear Peter had always felt for the old man grew and grew. The river, with all its dangers, was welcome. He had to get away quickly!

5

Peter crawled into his sleeping bag early, not to sleep, just to avoid being with the old man. Now that he knew Pickett had killed a man, everything he did took on added meaning. He remained awake thinking about tomorrow long after the old man had fed the animals and gone to his room. Peter heard him turn and toss and finally become quiet.

Solomon was in the pine tree talking softly to the night. For the first time in several days Lonesome, the coyote, sent his ringing call across the hills and down into the gorge. He heard the rattling of the tin pan and knew that Marty was eating.

He decided that he'd take off as soon as the old man left tomorrow morning. That should give him about a four-hour start if he wasn't missed before noon. If he did this right, he might allay the old man's suspicions and thus gain added time. He'd leave extra clothing and shoes in plain sight. He'd leave his sleeping bag on the bunk and take the extra they'd stored under the shelf in the pantry. He hoped Pickett would think he'd gone for a long hike and just hadn't got back for lunch. He might get as much as an extra two or three hours' start.

Peter was awakened by the old man lighting the fire and getting breakfast. For a few minutes he lay with his eyes shut, reviewing his plan.

They ate breakfast in silence. Afterward, Pickett was in no hurry to leave. He took two of the leftover biscuits out to Bill. The others he crumbled and scattered for the birds. Peter was nervous. He was ready to go. The old man stood for minutes in front of the cabin looking toward the river, then he stared up at the sky. Finally he looked up the mountain toward the snow line. At last he sauntered into the cabin.

Peter tried to ask casually, "You going to the diggings pretty soon?"

Pickett shook his head, "I'm through for the year. Finished the cleanup and put the sluice boxes away yesterday."

Peter's heart sank.

The old man puttered about the cabin. He took out the ashes, changed his bedding, then spent some time inspecting the food supply in the pantry. Finally he got out a can of grease and began greasing his shoes. He pointed at Peter's shoes, "Better grease 'em if you want 'em to last."

"I will," Peter said.

"Then do it."

Peter took off his shoes, greased them thoroughly under Pickett's watchful eyes, and put them on again.

53

Pickett leisurely finished his own shoes, humming under his breath. He got out the rifle, cleaned it, and tinkered with it for half an hour. Finally he loaded it, stuffed a handful of shells into his pocket, put on his old hat and coat, and went out. Peter watched him head up through the timber. Bill came from the shed and followed.

Peter knew he should wait at least half an hour to make sure the old man had really gone on some kind of hike. But he was too keyed up. He got the spare sleeping bag out and stuffed a dozen cans of food into it. Hastily, he made carrying straps with a length of rope and threw the sleeping bag over his shoulder. He slipped out into the nearby brush and ran for the river. He could no longer count on a four- or five-hour start. Pickett might return from his hike any minute and become suspicious.

The sleeping bag and canned goods were heavier than he'd planned. They forced him to lean forward for balance. But he was on his way home at last. He trotted along the shore until he reached the sheer canyon walls where the river plunged into the gorge. For a moment his courage deserted him. Then he stepped into the shallow water and waded to the first narrow, sandy beach.

Peter progressed from beach to beach as he had yesterday. He was trying to hurry, and he slipped and fell several times, going in once to his shoulders. He felt the fierce drag of the current reach for him. He grabbed for the jagged edge of a rock and climbed on top. He stood shaking with fright and cold. Slow down, he warned himself, this old river's just waiting.

Peter finally came to the long, straight stretch where he'd stopped yesterday. From here it was a new trail for him. He was tired and hungry. He rested a minute, then entered the water and began wading to the next beach. The water continued shallow, the current was not bad. Out in the middle it boomed along, kicking up five-foot waves with foaming tops. At the end of the straight stretch he sat on the extreme tip of the last beach to rest again and study the gorge ahead.

He was at the head of a bend he could see around. He'd have to wade. There were no more sandy beaches, but the shore was lined with big rocks that he could easily travel over. The walls of the canyon pinched in, forcing the river into a narrower trough through which it raced with endless thunder. The current increased noticeably in the shallow water where he walked. The sun stood directly overhead. It must be noon. Once again he thought of opening one of the cans of food, but rejected it because of the time eating would take.

Pickett should be returning to the cabin for lunch. Peter guessed he must have come about three miles. He had to put more distance between them.

Peter slipped his arms through the loops of the sleeping bag, stepped into the swift current, and began wading around the bend. The water grew deeper. It reached his hips, and he held his breath. The current was a solid force that slammed into him. Luckily, a change in the river bottom bent the channel toward the opposite shore. The water grew no deeper. A step at a time he edged around the bend and onto the rocks that lined the river's edge. By choosing his rocks carefully he made good time traveling. But jumping from rock to rock was tiring. He stopped to rest briefly. Ahead loomed another bend. The canyon walls rose sheer, as if sliced by a giant knife.

When he reached the bend, Peter stopped and studied the river. The current slammed into the sheer wall and bounced back toward the center of the channel with breath-catching speed. A half-dozen big boulders rose out of the channel. White water boiled around them.

Peter couldn't see around the bend, but if this current and the sounds up ahead which filled the gorge were any indication, it was not good. He had to get around this shoulder so he could see. From here he could tell the river ran deep at the point and with a speed no man could live through. It looked like his hike was going to end here. He felt discouraged and beat. He should have believed the old man.

He was turning back when his eyes found the small ledge in the face of the rock just above the waterline. It looked about three feet wide and followed the wall around the bend. It was no more than forty feet from where he stood. The water was not too deep to wade to it. The current was fast, but if he was careful. . . .

Peter let himself into the river slowly. It was a little above his knees. The current hit him with a force he'd never felt before. He clung to the rock and looked at the shelf and the racing water between. His courage wavered. If he fell here, he'd never regain his footing. He'd be swept into deep water in the full grip of that charging torrent. But he had to reach the ledge—or go back and be stuck for the next six months with a half-crazy old man.

He edged forward, feeling his way carefully over the rocky bottom. The water crept up his legs. The pressure of the current increased with the depth. When he was halfway to the ledge, it boiled around his hips. He leaned backward against its pull. He stopped and stood looking at the ledge. It was so near. A dozen feet more. Again he moved forward. The water grew no deeper. He was almost there. Another step. His hand was out reaching for a handhold on the ledge when a loose rock turned under his foot. He was thrown off balance, and he lunged for the ledge. His fingers struck, then the current snatched him away.

A giant's strength sucked him deep and tumbled him over and over. His lungs were bursting. He kicked and stroked wildly for the surface. He was tossed upward into sunlight, and he struck something solid. The force of the current pinned him momentarily against one of the huge boulders. Peter scrambled frantically for a handhold. His foot found a crevice. He heaved himself upward. The next moment, he sprawled across the flat surface face down, shaking and gagging.

Peter lay there several minutes, afraid to move. Then he carefully raised himself to hands and knees and looked about. The sleeping bag had been torn from his back. He thought he glimpsed it bobbing through the waves far downriver.

He was about forty or fifty feet out from the rock ledge and the white water between was a deep, tearing millrace. The boulder on which he lay was about two feet above water. The top was as big as a table. Looking further downriver, he could now see that this would have been as far as he could go. From here the river ran deep and swift right against the sheer walls of the canyon.

Peter discovered he could sit up safely, but the top was wet with spray and moss. He dared not stand. He sat hunched, shivering, thinking about his plight. He must not fall asleep, not even drowse, for fear he might roll off. He was marooned.

A wave of helplessness and fear claimed him. Then it passed, and he began thinking of Omar Pickett. Would the old man come looking for him, or would he figure Peter was good riddance and let him go? If he tried to follow, would he come this far? Or would he figure Peter had such a head start he could never catch him? There was no telling what that odd, cantankerous old man might do. How could he possibly help anyway?

Peter couldn't get warm. Cold spray kept drifting around him. A chill breeze poured down the canyon. He beat his arms and hugged them tight about his body for some faint warmth. A kingfisher flew down the gorge barely above the wave tops. A golden eagle dropped between the walls so low he could see its head turn as it searched for food.

The boy was ravenously hungry. He wondered how long he could stay on this rock without becoming weak from hunger or falling asleep and rolling off.

The sun finally passed from sight over the gorge. The shadow of the west wall crept over him. He was sitting hunched up, looking at nothing, when he heard the voice above the roar of the water.

"Boy! Boy!" There stood Pickett on the last rock, waving at him. He had a coil of rope looped over his lean shoulders.

Peter yelled at the top of his lungs, "Mr. Pickett! Mr. Pickett!" He started excitedly to his feet.

"Stay down!" the old man shouted. "Stay down!"

Peter sank back on all fours. He watched fearfully as Pickett calmly stepped off the rock into the swift current and edged toward the ledge. Water boiled against his long legs, but he seemed as sturdy as a tree trunk. He pulled himself up on the ledge, slipped the rope from his shoulders, held one end in his left hand and the coil in his right. "Get ready to catch," he shouted, "but don't stand up."

Pickett swung the coil around his head, then launched it out over the water with all his strength.

Peter watched the rope snake out, unrolling as it came. It was nylon and very light. The wind caught it and whipped it downriver. It fell into the water twenty feet short, long enough, but too light to carry all the way.

59

Pickett pulled the rope back, coiled it, and tried again. It fell further upriver but still a few feet short. Pickett tried twice more with the same results. He walked along the ledge, and Peter knew he was looking for a rock or stick to tie to the rope. The ledge was clean.

Pickett stood a moment, undecided, then began searching along the wall. He found a knob of rock, wound the rope about it, and tied it. The opposite end he knotted about his waist. Then he moved slowly back and forth along the ledge, studying the water. Finally, he stopped at a point above Peter. He took off his hat and coat and laid them on the ledge. Then he shed his old red shirt and boots.

Peter had a sudden suspicion and shouted at the top of his lungs, "You can't! You'll drown! Stay there, Mr. Pickett. Stay there!"

The old man stood tall and lean, long arms hanging at his sides, white hair flying. Peter shouted again, "Don't, Mr. Pickett! You can't make it. Don't try!"

Pickett didn't answer or even look up. He moved along the ledge a few feet, stopped, then moved again. He stood a moment looking at the water. Suddenly he launched his lean body straight out into the current in a mighty leap.

He disappeared from sight.

Peter half rose to his feet, felt them slip on the slick surface, and sank back on all fours. His eyes swept the water.

The white head bobbed up and hurtled toward him.

Pickett had calculated well. He'd jumped at the very spot where the current could carry him to the rock. A moment later, he struck. Peter grabbed his arm with both hands and began to pull. In seconds, Pickett lay gasping and coughing on the rock beside him.

Pickett turned his head and grinned at Peter. "Kind of chilly place you've got here. How about goin' ashore where it's warm and dry?"

Peter tried to smile. His throat was thick. He finally managed, "Whenever you say."

"Good!" Pickett sat up, untied the rope from about his middle, and pulled in the slack. He looped the rope around Peter and tied it. He tied the end about himself. "In case the rope slips through our hands, we're tied fast," he explained. "That rock we're anchored to is good and solid."

"What if the rope breaks?" Peter was thinking of both of them tied to this small line.

"It's guaranteed to stand sixteen hundred pounds' pull. The river won't be half that. But if it busts, I'll demand my money back," he grinned. "We'll jump in. When the rope tightens and holds, the current will start workin' for us," he explained. "It'll act as a lever and swing us toward the ledge. But climb the rope hand over hand as much as you can to help. When you reach the ledge, grab hold and climb up. All right. Ready?"

Peter nodded. His mouth was dry.

"When I say 'Jump,' we go together. Jump straight out toward shore as far as you can."

Peter sucked air into his lungs. His hands, gripping the rope, were clammy.

Pickett said sharply, "Now! Jump!"

Peter shut his eyes, lunged erect, and leaped as far as he could. Icy water closed over him. The rope tightened with a jerk that almost cut him in two. His lungs screamed for air. The next moment he was tossed to the surface.

"Keep goin'!" Pickett's voice shouted behind him. "Pull! Keep pullin'!"

Peter began pulling himself up the rope hand over hand. A wave splashed over his head. He swallowed water. Current jerked him under before he could catch a breath. He shot to the surface to hear the old man's voice shouting, "Pull, boy! Pull! Pull!"

His arms ached. The rope was slick with water, and his hands slipped. He slid down and slammed into Pickett. He grabbed the rope again and pulled himself upward with all his strength. Then the current slammed him hard against the rock wall. The ledge was just above his eyes. He lunged upward, found a handhold. A big hand boosted him from behind, and he sprawled on the ledge. The next moment, Omar Pickett rolled up beside him.

For several minutes they lay side by side, gagging, spitting water, and getting their breath back.

Finally Omar Pickett sat up, leaned his back against the rock wall, and wiped water from his eyes. "We made it," he said. "By golly, we made it! Not many

62

jump into this old river and get out again—and that's a fact. You all right, boy?"

Peter rolled over. He looked up at the soft blue strip of sky. He felt the good, solid rock beneath him. He listened to the thunder of the thwarted river. Peter felt he'd been dead and now lived again. "I'm fine," he said, smiling at Omar Pickett, "I'm just fine."

He sat up and looked at the old man beside him. The white hair, still dripping water, was plastered to his head. His heavy underwear, that Peter's father called long johns, was soaked to his lean body. He looked thinner, more like a scarecrow than ever.

Peter said simply, "You saved my life, Mr. Pickett. I'll never forget. But you took an awful chance, jumping into the river. You could have drowned."

Pickett looked at him thoughtfully, "How did you figure to get off that rock, boy?"

Peter shook his head. "I don't know. I couldn't think any more. But because I did a dumb thing is no reason you should risk your life. I'm glad you did though," he smiled.

Omar Pickett's gray eyes squinted at Peter. "You're quite a boy, and that's a fact." He rose stiffly, "Let's get these two old canyon rats out of here before they catch their death of pneumonia." He untied the rope about his middle and put on his boots, shirt, coat, and old floppy hat. He unfastened the rope from the rock and tied the end around himself again. "We'll stay tied together until we pass the jumpin' rocks going back.

63

I'll go first. If I slip and fall, you can hold me with the rope. If you fall, I'll do the same. When the current hits, you lean into it, bend your upstream leg and straighten the downstream one, and push against the water with it. All right, here goes."

Pickett slipped off the ledge almost hip deep into the river. The current boiled against his legs, but he leaned into it and moved ahead. Peter payed out the line, but it wasn't needed. Omar Pickett made the rock, turned, and waved Peter to come on.

Peter lowered himself into the river and did exactly as Pickett had told him. He reached the rock with no trouble. They made their way upstream together. At the first sandy beach, the old man untied the rope and looped it about his shoulders again. They walked back against the rock wall where a cleft at the top let a ray of late sun into the canyon, and they sat down in its warmth to rest.

Pickett leaned back, removed his hat, and heaved a sigh, "Sun sure feels mighty good after the river. We'll rest a bit. But we can't sit here long in these wet clothes."

"I lost the sleeping bag and about a dozen cans of food," Peter said.

"We've got another sleepin' bag, and the pantry's full of food."

"It was lucky you brought the rope."

"It's the best piece of equipment you can carry here in the canyon."

Peter felt almost drowsy in the warm sun, but his

mind could not let go of the amazing afternoon's happening. "You must have started looking for me as soon as you got back to the cabin."

"Just about." Pickett had shut his eyes and lifted his leathery face to let the late sun beat down on it. "I was suspicious right off. You'd never been late for lunch before. You went up to the snow line and checked because you thought I'd lied to you about how deep it was and how rough the goin'. You discovered you couldn't get out that way. Downriver is the only other way out of here. When I found the spare sleepin' bag gone, I knew where you were headed."

Pickett stretched his long legs luxuriously. "You got further than I figured you would. I thought you'd be scared out where the rock walls begin and the river enters the gorge again. I expected to find you sittin' on the beach waitin' for me. But you made the rock shelf. That's the limit anyone can go on foot. It peters out around that bend. Then you've got a full mile of water, swift as a race horse and a hundred feet deep, with an eighth of a mile of rapids at the end. I wouldn't have believed you could get that far. You did fine. But one bad slip anywhere along this three miles of river and you could have drowned."

"I almost did. And I'd still be trapped on that rock but for you. I was a fool to try," Peter confessed.

"You was a boy wantin' to get home mighty bad. I should have thought about that instead of bein' mad because you intruded on my privacy."

"I'm sorry."

65

"I believe you," the old man smiled. "I had time to do a lotta thinkin' while I was comin' down here lookin' for you." He dug a heel thoughtfully in the sand. "Man can live alone so long he don't consider anybody or anythin' but himself, and that's a fact. But the important thing before this meetin' is—do you believe me now? Or am I going to chase over this country every few days lookin' for you?"

"I believe you. You won't have to look for me again." Peter thought of the months here if a plane didn't come, and a great loneliness went crying through him.

Pickett said gently, "The time'll go faster if you don't think about it, boy."

"Didn't you ever get homesick out here alone?" Peter asked.

"I like to died at first."

"Why didn't you leave?"

Pickett squeezed water from the cuffs of his shirt, then squinted at the sun. Finally he said thoughtfully, "You don't always think straight when you're young. I didn't figure I had a choice." He rose abruptly and jammed the old hat down on his wet hair. The sharp, gray eyes regarded Peter. "The name," he said, "is Omar."

"Mine's Peter."

"Then what say we be gettin' back, Pete. It'll get cold soon as that sun drops outa sight, and I'm so hungry my belly thinks my throat's cut."

Peter felt that the wall between them had broken

66

down. He no longer feared or disliked Omar Pickett. The old man had risked his life to save him. So Omar was a little odd with his tame owl, deer, and marten. There was no harm in that. By his own admission, he'd killed a man. He'd praised the dead man, called him a friend, and a brave man. He tended the grave carefully. Omar Pickett was no ordinary murderer. There had to be a logical explanation. But that, Peter knew, might always be Omar's secret.

6

Peter was up and dressed before Omar. For the first time, he got the fire going and the cabin warmed up. But there was still no sound from the bedroom. Carefully, he opened the door and looked in. Omar lay on his back, eyes open, staring at the ceiling.

Peter asked, "You all right, Omar?"

Omar turned his head, "Been tryin' to work up nerve enough to get up for some time. Haven't got it yet. I've been listenin' to you scramblin' around out there. First time anybody ever got the fire goin' and the room warm for me to get up in." He stretched long arms and smiled. "Mighty great luxury. Wouldn't take much of this to spoil me rotten, and that's the truth."

"Is there anything wrong?"

"Sore. I got a whole bunch of aches. I found I got muscles I didn't know I had. Guess the river and that big rock bunged me up more'n I thought. How you feelin'?"

"A little stiff. I've got a couple of sore spots. But that's all."

"Nothin' like bein' a boy," Omar murmured. "Bounce back like a rubber ball. Was a time I did that, too. Now I got about as much bounce as a rock." He rubbed a hand over his bony chest. "Hurts to take a deep breath. I bruised some muscles pretty bad, maybe cracked a couple ribs."

"Can I do anything?"

"It hurts to try to sit up. Maybe if you got on the bed behind me, you could sort of push against my back and shoulders, and I could make it without strainin' these sore muscles."

Peter did as Omar instructed. Groaning and catching his breath, the old man finally sat upright on the edge of the bed and began to dress. He could not bend over, so Peter put his shoes on and laced them.

Omar hobbled into the kitchen and sat down stiffly. "Guess you'll have to do the cookin'," he said.

"Tell me what to do."

"You want biscuits or pancakes for breakfast?"

"We've been having biscuits," Peter said. "How about pancakes for a change? That is, if you'd like them, too."

"Fine. I like pancakes—no bones. Get the crock of sourdough down."

"But that's for biscuits."

"Biscuits, cake, bread, doughnuts, cookies, pancakes. You name it," Omar said. "Why, Pete, without sourdough they might never have settled the West."

Peter looked at him sharply.

"A small exaggeration," Omar admitted, "but not

69

much. In the early days, every farm kitchen had its sourdough crock. And whole meals were often planned around the things a woman could do with sourdough. Every prospector, miner, trapper, and sheepherder carried his sourdough with him, buried right in the flour sack. You know how old that crock of dough is? Almost fifty years. I started it right after I came out here to live."

"And it doesn't spoil?"

"Nope. When you take out a cup, you add a cup of flour and water each time. So you keep renewin' it. You let it set twenty-four hours to work, and you're ready to go again. Now, take out half a cup of that starter and put it in a bowl."

At Omar's direction Peter added powdered egg, pancake mix, powdered milk, water, and oil.

Omar decided they should open one of the small cans of ham to celebrate their escape from the river. There was coffee for Omar and chocolate made with powdered milk and water for Peter. It was a fine breakfast, and Peter prepared it all. It was the first time in his life he'd ever cooked anything.

There was nothing wrong with Omar's appetite. He leaned back finally, sighed, and patted his stomach. "So help me Hannah! You got the makin's of a good cook," he said, "and that's a fact. Don't know when I've enjoyed a breakfast more."

"I'll do the dishes. Why don't you go out in the sun?"

Omar made his way outside and sat down on a

70

block of wood that lay close to the cabin wall. He leaned back, stretched his long legs before him, and bared his chest to the sun's rays. Bill came from the shed and nuzzled him.

Peter called, "You got any tobacco?"

"No," Omar said, "it's in the pantry in a gallon coffee can."

The coffee can was almost full of plugs about two and a half inches square. He took out one and gave it to Omar.

Bill looked at Peter and began to shake his horns.

"You want to feed 'im?" Omar asked.

"No," Peter said.

"You don't like Bill, eh?"

"I don't like him, and he doesn't like me."

"Happens," Omar said. "Animals got their likes and dislikes the same as people." He tore small bits off the plug and fed them to Bill.

Peter returned to the kitchen and cleaned up the breakfast dishes.

Bill finished the tobacco, got his petting, then wandered off among the trees.

When Peter went out, he glanced automatically at the empty sky as he'd been doing for days. He checked his fire pile to be sure it was still ready to explode into flames at the touch of the lighter. Satisfied, he returned, sat on the ground near Omar, and leaned against the wall. Omar was watching him and smiling.

Peter said stubbornly, "A plane still could come." He asked hopefully, "Couldn't it, Omar?"

71

"Of course," Omar said. "Absolutely. Let's see. How long's it been now?"

Peter figured. "A week today." It didn't seem possible it was that long. "My father won't quit," he insisted. "He'll keep looking." But he knew planes must have flown their flight plan a dozen times by now. Gloom overwhelmed him.

Omar said, "It only takes one plane goin' over once to spot us, Pete. But with seven days gone, the chances are gettin' pretty slim. Don't pin all your hopes on a plane. The main thing is you're alive and healthy. Come spring, you'll go out none the worse for wear. Tell yourself this's just goin' to be one long vacation."

Peter nodded, "But if there is a chance, I don't want to miss it."

"Of course you don't." Omar eased his shoulders against the log wall and changed the subject. "You said your dad owned some kind of company?"

"Grayson Electronics. He manufactures special electrical equipment. He just bought an air-conditioning company and a company that manufactures a saw that can cut through concrete."

"Sounds like a big man," Omar said. "We used to call 'em captains of industry. Don't know what they call 'em now."

Peter told Omar about his home, how his mother disliked the trophy room, the "horn room," she called it. He talked about his school and confessed he was nothing at sports—too light and thin.

"I used to be skinny like you," Omar said. "Don't worry. The weight and muscle will come."

Peter asked, "Where's your family, Omar? Were you born around here?"

"A little over a hundred miles from here. No brothers or sisters. Any relatives I had must be dead now. I've lived out here almost fifty years. I'm what you'd call a canyon rat."

"Was the cabin here when you came?"

Omar shook his head, smiling as he thought back. "Wasn't a thing. Not a blessed thing. I built the cabin myself in one summer. Just like it is now."

"You mean, this is what you always wanted?"

"Nope. Started out to be a guide when I was young. It didn't work out, so I came up here. I'd guided into this country and knew about this spot and liked it. I wanted to be alone. I don't know any place you can be more alone than right here."

"You've got friends downriver, in the towns?"

Omar shook his head. "Know some people, jet-boat skippers and a few others. Wouldn't exactly call any of 'em friends, though. My friends are here." He waved an arm. "This river, the land, the trees, the canyon, and everything in it. The animals and birds just moved over a little to make room for me to live with 'em. We get along fine."

"What do you do besides live here and mine a little gold?" Peter asked.

"Why, I watch over the wildlife in the canyon and

that forest that stretches up back of the cabin. Now and then I help an animal that gets into trouble. Like Bill. I found him when he was a little spotted fawn. A cougar had killed his mother and he was starving to death. I bottle-fed him. That's why he's so tame. I found Solomon with a busted wing and splinted it up. I don't know how many deer, elk, coyote pups, owls, golden eagles, and even a bear cub or two I've patched up and turned loose the past fifty years. This country and these animals are mine. Course that's not so," he said smiling. "The animals're wild, and the land belongs to the government. But after all these years, I figure I've got some squatter's rights."

"Do you take out much gold from your diggings?"

"Thousand or two, dependin' on how hard I work. That buys everythin' I need, with some left over."

"I've never seen a gold mine," Peter said.

"Give me a few days to work out these stiff kinks and we'll take a hike around."

Omar's recovery was not speedy. He decided he'd broken no ribs, only bruised them. But the river had given his lean old frame a beating. He fed Solomon and Bill, but made no effort to do anything else. Peter took over running the cabin. He was first up in the morning, and got the fire going and the room warm. He prepared all meals while Omar sat at the table, directing every move. He cleaned up the cabin and split and carried in all the wood. He even sliced the jerky into the tin plate for Marty at night and set it inside the door for him. But no matter what he was doing, his ears were always tuned to the sound of a plane motor. He never stepped outside but his eyes went first to the sky.

Peter now saw a completely different Omar Pickett. The old man was cheerful, good-natured. He said once, "If I'd known company could be this good, I'd have got somebody in here long ago. But then," he added thoughtfully, "they might not been as easy to get along with as you are."

They decided to go fishing because Omar was fish-hungry. "We can fish in the river right here in front of the cabin," he said. "You'll be close to your fire pile if a plane should pop over the mountains or come shootin' up the gorge. But you'll have to do the fishin'. I don't feel up to standin' on a rock and swingin' a pole yet."

"I've never caught a fish," Peter said.

"Then your education's not only been neglected, you haven't even lived yet. Come on."

They used grubs that Omar said were good for fish up here. Omar showed Peter how to fasten them on the hook so the fast water wouldn't rip them off. Omar sat on the bank and directed Peter where to cast and how to handle the pole. "Don't run out too much line," he cautioned. "That's plenty for a beginner. Now make your cast so you lay your hook just beyond that rock where the water's slack. You just might find a goofang restin' there."

"A what?"

"You never heard of a goofang? Well, he looks like

a trout, only different, and he's about the size of a trout, only bigger. Don't be surprised if you hook 'im in the tail because he always swims backward to keep the water out of his eyes."

Peter looked at him.

"S'fact! Just keep that grub moving around the rock, and be ready if you hook one."

It took three casts to land the lure where Omar said it should be. After about twenty minutes, Peter hooked something. The line yanked taut, the pole bent almost double. His heart jumped into his throat as the line ripped through the water.

"Reel 'im in!" Omar shouted. "Reel 'im, Pete! Reel 'im in. Don't give 'im slack."

With Omar shouting advice, Peter worked the fish into shallow water and landed him on the bank. He unhooked it and handed it to Omar. "Is this a goofang?" he asked.

Omar inspected the twelve-inch fish soberly, "Afraid not. This here's a genuine rainbow trout. Try again."

Over the next hour Peter managed to land three more nice ones, though he lost as many.

"Might as well call it a day," Omar said. "This's all we can eat."

As they made their way slowly to the cabin Peter asked, "Are there any other queer fish in the river beside goofangs?"

"Sure," Omar said. "Now you take the log gar. He's a big fish about as long as from here to there. His snout's studded with teeth like a saw. He can saw right

76

through a big log. They've ruined lots of good logs by cuttin' 'em up fine as stove wood. If a log gar catches a man in the water he can make mincemeat of him. Lots of loggers been killed by log gars. And then there's the whirligig fish. It always swims in circles. In winter, you bore a hole through the ice and smear the edges of the hole with grease. They smell the grease and swim around and around the rim of the hole until they fly right out on the ice and you can gather 'em up. The upland trout, of course, is different. It nests in trees and never goes near the water. Funny thing about that fish. It builds its nest upside down."

"I think I'll stick to trout," Peter said, smiling.

Omar nodded soberly, "I would, if I was you."

The fifth morning, Omar announced that he felt almost as good as new. "Most of the kinks are out," he said. "Suppose we take a turn up through the timber for a look around."

Peter hesitated, "I'd like to."

"How long's it been now, Pete?"

"Today's the twelfth day."

"I never knew an all-out search to go more than two weeks."

"Then I've got two more days," Peter said stubbornly. "You said it only took one plane flying over once to spot us."

"That's right," Omar agreed. "While you hold down the fort, I'll take a hike up through the woods."

Peter watched him go off through the trees. Bill came from the shed and trotted after him.

For the next two days Peter stayed close to the cabin and his fire pile. But no plane came.

The third morning, Peter watched as Omar put on coat and hat and loaded the old rifle. "You going out again?" he asked.

"Thought I'd take a swing past the diggin's, then up to the snow line to check on the deer and elk. They'll start workin' down toward the river as the snow line gets lower."

"Will we have snow here later on?"

"A foot, maybe more. Enjoy what good weather's left, Pete. It won't last much longer."

Peter frowned, biting his lips. "If a plane came and didn't see us, would it likely fly over here more than once?"

"Of course. Over rough country like this I'd say they'd crisscross it several times to make sure they'd seen everythin'."

"Would there be time to get back to light the signal fire?"

"Between the first and second passes there could be as much as an hour."

"Then I'm going with you."

"You'd better see what I get up at the diggin's first. Then you'll have some idea what it's all about." Omar went into the bedroom and returned with a two-quart jar almost full of gold nuggets and fine flakes. He handed it to Peter. "Be careful. It's heavy."

It weighed like lead. Peter held it and admired the gold. "Gee! I've never seen gold like this before. All

78

I've seen was in rings and watches and things. How much is there here?"

"About twenty-five hundred dollars' worth. I worked longer and took out more than usual this summer."

Peter turned the jar, watching the golden particles shift and flow. "What will you use it for? Grub and things like that?"

"Not this gold." Omar's voice sounded tough. "This goes to fight that Mountain Home Loggin' outfit."

"You mean the one that wants to come in here and log all this timber?"

"That's the one."

"How will you fight them?"

"Go out next spring with the first jet boat and hire a lawyer and let him do it somehow."

"This gold won't go far," Peter said. "If they're big, like you say, they can spend all kinds of money to fight you."

"I've got a couple thousand more in the bank."

"Even that won't be a starter."

"I don't figure to lick 'em," Omar admitted. "I just want to bring the facts out in the open where everybody can see 'em. I hear there's lots of people and organizations that're interested in things like savin' wild game and protectin' the rivers and forests and such. I'm hopin' some of them will take notice of these facts and jump in and help fight."

"You'll have lost all your money," Peter pointed out.

"I know," Omar agreed. "But somebody's got to start fightin' 'em. This country's given me a good life. I owe it somethin'. The land, timber, river, and the wild animals here can't fight for their lives. So somebody else has got to do it for them, even if it's only an old canyon rat like me." He took the jar from Peter's hands and returned it to the bedroom. "Put a couple hunks of jerky in your pocket to chew and let's go. You haven't really seen this country yet."

They headed downriver, following the faint trail that Omar had worn over the years. Peter realized suddenly they were going to go right past the mysterious grave. A minute later, he caught a glimpse of the pile of rocks and the small cross through the trees. He glanced at it as they passed. Omar looked straight ahead.

7

Peter was disappointed in the diggings. There was little to see, just two sluice boxes, troughs a little over a foot wide and about fourteen feet long with thin cross-pieces nailed on the bottom. The boxes lay under a pole shed for the winter.

"Is this all of it?" Peter asked.

"What'd you expect?"

"I thought there'd be a hole and wheelbarrows and things like that."

"This's a placer mine," Omar explained. "That means you wash the gravel in the creek to get the gold that's collected there. I put the boxes in the creek so the water runs through, then shovel gravel into them and wash it. The gold, if any, catches in those little cross-baffles."

"That's all it takes?"

"That and a strong back. Well, let's head up and look around."

They began climbing toward the snow line. Omar's long legs swung along easily. The rifle was slung carelessly over his shoulder. He was smiling, happy. His eyes missed nothing. He began to whistle softly, a rollicking, lively tune. The sound carried through the silence. The tune was one Peter remembered faintly. He said, surprised, "I thought you wanted to see the deer and elk and things."

"Do."

"But you're scaring them."

Omar shook his head, "I'm just lettin' them know I'm comin'. Otherwise, they'd be startled when they suddenly spotted us. They'd take off. Game'll usually see you first when you're movin' around. I whistle and sing to sorta keep myself company. You learn to do a lotta things to entertain yourself out here when you're alone."

Omar continued to whistle a few bars every couple of hundred yards. Peter finally asked, "What's that tune, Omar?"

"An old one my daddy taught me. You probably never heard of it. It's called 'The Big Rock Candy Mountains.'"

"I've heard of it. Do you know the words?"

"I used to know a few. But I mostly whistle, 'cause my singin's the kind that sours the milk."

"I'd like to hear the words."

"Well, okay," Omar said. "Remember, you asked for it. It's a hobo tellin' his friends about the paradise he's goin' to." Omar began to sing in a thin, reedy voice:

"I'm headin' for a land that's far away,
Beside the crystal fountains.
I'll see you all this coming fall
In The Big Rock Candy Mountains."

"Had enough?" Omar asked.
"What's the next one?" Peter asked. "I like it."

"In The Big Rock Candy Mountains,
There's a land that's fair and bright,
Where the handouts grow on bushes
And you sleep out every night.
Where the boxcars all are empty
And the sun shines ev'ry day—
Oh, the birds and the bees and the cigarette trees,
The lemonade springs where the blue bird sings,
In The Big Rock Candy Mountains."

"Sing another one," Peter begged. "Sing another,
Omar."
"You mean you can take more?" Omar asked.
"Well, here goes:"

"In The Big Rock Candy Mountains,
All the cops have wooden legs,
And the bulldogs all have rubber teeth,
And the hens lay soft-boiled eggs.
The farmers' trees are full of fruit,
And the barns are full of hay.

Oh, I'm bound to go where there ain't no snow,
Where the sleet don't fall and the wind don't blow,
In The Big Rock Candy Mountains.

In The Big Rock Candy Mountains,
The jails are made of tin. . . ."

A blasting sound up ahead made Peter jump. It began on a low, bellowing note that rose to a shrill, angry scream. "What was that?" he whispered fearfully.

"Bull elk buglin'."

The sound came again, nearer, piercing, menacing and angry.

"Come on," Omar said. "There's a little glade up here. With luck, you're gonna see somethin'."

Peter had to trot to keep up with Omar's long legs. The bugling came twice more before Omar hauled up behind a bush. Peter peeked around him and looked into a small clearing. A half-dozen cow elk were clustered in the center. A huge bull stood a few feet from them. As Peter looked, the bull stretched his neck and sent a shrill scream echoing through the forest. It was answered almost immediately from the nearby trees.

"This old feller here is tellin' the world this's his harem and he's not about to stand for any interference from anybody," Omar whispered. "That other'n's sayin', 'I'm a better fighter than you are, old man, and I'm comin' to prove it.'"

Omar had scarcely finished when the second bull

84

walked into view. The newcomer was almost as large as the first. The two advanced toward each other, heads outstretched. They stopped a few feet apart and warily circled. Then, as though on signal, they stopped circling and charged. They came together with a resounding clash of antlers. They pushed and twisted, digging their feet into the earth as they tried to throw each other. Clods of dirt and grass flew up from their flying hoofs. They battled on even terms. Then they backed off, glaring. They came together again with such force, Peter expected their antlers to splinter. The older began driving the younger bull back, sliding and slipping. With a twist of his head, the herd monarch brought the young bull stumbling to his knees. He backed off and charged into the downed bull's side, hooking viciously with his horns. The young bull scrambled to his feet and ran off into the brush.

The old bull stood a minute glaring after his foe, then he walked majestically to the cows and led them from the meadow.

Omar said, "Gettin' pretty late in the season for fightin'. If that old bull had spotted us, he might have charged in his frame of mind. That could have happened to you when you was rammin' around up here alone. A mad bull elk is nothing to fool with, and that's a fact."

"I believe it," Peter said.

They continued up through the trees, and finally Peter said, "You didn't finish that song."

"I guess the bull fight startled it right outa me,"

Omar said. "I don't know much more." But he began
to sing softly:

"In The Big Rock Candy Mountains,
The jails are made of tin,
And you can bust right out again
As soon as they put you in.
There ain't no short-handled shovels,
No axes, saws, or picks—
I'm a-goin to stay where you sleep all day—
Oh, they boiled in oil the inventor of toil
In The Big Rock Candy Mountains.

Oh, come with me, and we'll go see
The Big Rock Candy Mountains."

"I liked that, Omar," Peter said. "You've got to
teach me the words."
"Sure," Omar said. "Any time."
In the distance, a pair of deer stood perfectly still
under a tree. They flapped their big ears and watched
the boy and man pass. A little further, Omar pointed
to a track in the soft earth like a man's big hand. "That
old bear better look for a hole mighty quick or snow's
gonna catch him." A small band of elk wandered leisurely away. A single buck, that looked as big as Bill,
tossed up his head and walked off unhurriedly. Squirrels and chipmunks darted about on the ground and
raced through the tree branches. A pair of pheasants
exploded out of the grass under their feet. A covey of

chukars fled down hill, weaving through the trees. Jays scolded at them. A flock of crows went over, talking companionably.

Peter said, "I never saw so many different kinds of birds and animals. And they don't seem to be afraid of us."

"A lot of people don't get back in here because it's too hard travelin'. This's the forest primeval, Pete. I like to think it's been like this since time began."

"I'll bet it has," Peter said. "These animals don't even scare at your singing. I get the feeling they sort of like it."

"I could take offense at that," Omar said, scowling.

Peter laughed and asked, "Do you know any more songs?"

"A few," Omar said. "I whistle 'Down in the Valley' some. The way I do it sounds like some kind of bird callin', I guess. Maybe that makes the animals curious and they wait around to see what it is."

"Do you know the words?"

"There's a mess of verses. I know a couple. I'm not sure if you'd like them, though."

"I'd like to hear what you know. Sing it anyway, Omar."

Omar began to sing:

"Down in the valley, valley so low,
Hang your head over, hear the wind blow.
Hear the wind blow, dear.
Hear the wind blow.

Hang your head over,
Hear the wind blow.

Writing this letter containing three lines,
Answer my question: Will you be mine?
Will you be mine, dear. Will you be mine?
Answer my question: Will you be mine?

Build me a castle, forty feet high,
So I can see her as she goes by;
As she goes by, dear, as she goes by,
So I can see her as she goes by."

"I like it," Peter said. "I've never heard anything like it. Do you know any modern songs, Omar?"

Omar shook his head. "How'd I learn 'em way out here? Now and then, when I go to town, I hear one. Can't remember 'em, though. Anyhow, these oldies seem more appropriate for up here." His eyes crinkled as he grinned at Peter. "I ain't sung those songs in I don't know how many years; always whistled 'em. Didn't even know if I'd remember the words. I'd likely never sung 'em again if it hadn't been for you."

They hit the snow line and began wading in snow. The wildlife disappeared, and Omar stopped singing. "They're beginnin' to work lower," he explained. "They'll keep ahead of the snow until they're right down to the river."

They began following a ridge that Omar called a hogback. The climbing was hard and steep. "Place up here I want you to see," Omar panted.

They stopped once to rest but came out finally on a high, sheer finger of rock that rose several hundred feet above the forest floor.

They were out from under the trees with the great bowl of the sky above them. Peter's eyes immediately turned up.

"No plane?" Omar asked.

"No." The air up here was damp and keen and very clear. Peter looked down on the forest through which they'd just passed. The treetops were a green carpet undulating to hills and valleys and ravines. Far below, the rock-brown slash of the river's gorge edged the green. He could not see the cabin, but he knew where it was. A golden eagle rode the air currents down there as he cruised at treetop level. A cold breeze came off the high snow fields, and Peter followed its passage as it ruffled the trees on the way to the river.

The forest flowed around the base of the rock and rose tier on tier into the sky above them. The great weight of the timber mass and the amazing variety of wildlife it sheltered bore down on Peter. "I didn't know it was anything like this," he said. "It doesn't look so big from the cabin or when you're hiking through it."

"You're seein' a tiny corner," Omar explained. "This's one of the greatest virgin stands left in the state, maybe the greatest. It goes up over these high ridges. Then fans out and follows the gorge and river for miles." He waved a long arm, smiling, and said, "The 'hills of home,' Pete. I've known these mountains almost from the day I was born. All I want is to live here, to sort of watch over the animals, see the eagle and hawk soar, listen to the coyotes' yappin' in the dead of night, watch the salmon fight their way up to spawn, the geese and ducks migrate. Why, I've seen some of these trees grow from saplin's, like the big pile in front of the cabin. Feller I know in town once said, 'Omar, you're missin' a lot of livin', holed up out there in that canyon.' Maybe. But when I look around the towns, I don't figure I've missed anything important."

"This right here is the timber and land that logging company wants?" Peter asked.

"Mountain Home Loggin' Company," Omar said. "They want the timber. They couldn't care less about the land. If they get in here, you won't know this country when they're through with it. There won't hardly be a bush or tree of any kind left standing."

"Do they have to ruin it all just to get the big timber out?"

"That's the way they operate. Clear-cutting, they call it. There's places you can use that method, but not on slopes and mountains like this."

"What do they do that's so bad?" Peter asked.

"They bulldoze in a regular network of loggin' roads to get the timber out, then they slash everything that grows. They practically scalp the land. When they finish, this'll be a barren wasteland of stumps, mountains of slashings, ripped-up brush and downed trees they've left behind. Deer, elk, birds—all game will disappear because there won't be enough left to feed a gopher and no place for the wildlife to hide."

Peter looked down on the great stand of timber and found Omar's picture hard to believe. "You're sure that's how it will be?" he asked.

"They've been doing it the same way since they came from the East almost a hundred years ago. That leopard's not gonna change his spots unless he has to. They're big and rich, Pete. They're interested in only one thing. Makin' money. They come in, get the timber the quickest, cheapest way possible, and get out, leavin' the mess behind. 'Cut-out and get-out.'

"I can show you a place similar to this that they logged about thirty years ago. When they first wanted to go in there, they got opposition from people who knew how they logged. So they came up with a big propaganda story about how careful, how select they'd be. They'd take only the mature trees and let the others develop for future harvestin'. They convinced a lot of people they'd be there so long that their kids might go to work for them, loggin' in that very stand of timber. Well, they logged it.

"Flat Iron Creek's about forty-five or fifty miles downriver. You go past a corner of it in a jet boat. I decided I'd go down and log for them. I wasn't doin' anything else."

Omar shook his head. "I'd never seen such out-and-out destruction. Flat Iron Creek was a big, beautiful, virgin stand. There was all kinds of animals and birds.

The creek was one of the finest salmon-spawnin' and trout streams around, clean and crystal clear. They logged right to the stream bank. They dragged logs through the stream over the spawnin' beds while the salmon were spawnin'. The salmon scattered, then came back and laid their eggs, and the men dragged more logs through and destroyed the eggs. A couple of places they blocked the stream bed with junk, and the creek had to cut a new channel. I saw trees fall with golden eagle nestlings. Some baby birds were killed, others went floppin' across the ground with broken legs and wings. They put in a network of roads, and when it rained, the water ran down the roads into the creek, carryin' mud with it. The spawnin' beds were covered so deep they were destroyed.

"I stuck it out a week and quit. That was my first and last loggin'."

"That sounds awful," Peter said.

Omar nodded. "It went on for four years, then that loggin' job which Mountain Home had promised would last from one generation into the next was over. They had scalped the land clean as a hound's tooth and left. I was told that hunters used to go in there, drive up and down the loggin' roads, and use the little game that was left for target practice.

"Today it still looks like a war'd been fought there. There's no game except a few rabbits, gophers, and sage hens. And the creek's a bone-dry rock bed. The salmon run's gone forever. The people responsible for that are mostly dead now. I hope they fry in hell a thousand years."

Peter was aghast at the thought of such destruction. But the stream loss puzzled him. "Why would the stream dry up? It rains and snows as much as ever," he pointed out. "That's what makes streams, isn't it?"

"Without trees and ground cover, the water runs off like off a roof. This forest ground," Omar explained, "is a mass of roots; some big, some so little you can hardly see 'em. Those roots not only feed the plants they're attached to, but durin' heavy rains and spring thaws, they act like strainers, holdin' the soil in place while letting the water gradually escape. Without that network, water pours down the slopes and mountains in a flood for a few days or weeks. It takes the good topsoil with it. In loggin' Flat Iron Creek, those roots and the ground cover were destroyed. You wouldn't believe the gullies that have been washed in that land. This'll be the same. Another wasteland."

"How can you be so sure?"

"They're the same kind of mountainous country. They have very poor soil. It's taken maybe a thousand years to grow this forest like it is. Once it's logged off the Mountain Home way, it'll go like Flat Iron Creek. There's maybe a dozen good streams and any number of small ones draining this timber stand. A lot of those will dry up, others will become trickles." Omar was silent a moment, staring out over the tops of the forest. "That river," he said finally, waving his arm, "looks big and powerful, and it is. You and I know that. But it's also very delicate. What affects the smallest trickle, the smallest stream, affects the river because they make the river."

"Maybe if this logging company understood, . . ." Peter began.

"They've known for more than half a century. Their business is makin' money. And they do it. They've got a good argument to keep people from complainin' too much. They say, 'We're makin' jobs for hundreds. You can't stop progress.' Some progress I can do without! But they do make jobs for three, four, five years in an area. When the timber's gone, so's the jobs, and so is Mountain Home Loggin' Company. The mess stays for all time."

"You mean they don't clean it up or anything?" Peter asked.

"Never, Pete. You should've seen 'em when they came in here last spring." Omar said thoughtfully. "A big jet-boat load of 'em and Mr. James T. Sutton, Junior, the owner. They spread out through this forest like a bunch of locusts while James T. sat on a rock like the lord of creation and waited for them to report to him. I knew old Jim Senior, his father. He was a big, beefy, domineerin' man, tough as a railroad spike. Junior's a carbon copy. I knew it was no use, but I tried to explain to him that this land couldn't be clear-cut. He didn't even look at me once while I talked. When I finished, he got up and walked off."

"He didn't say anything?"

Omar shook his head. "What's an old canyon rat know about makin' money."

"There must be some way to stop him," Peter said hotly. "This forest belongs to the country, doesn't it? The people should have a say."

"That's what me and my little jar of gold dust aim to find out, come spring." He smiled at Peter. "Sure glad you're here to boil over to. Been holdin' that in a long time. Well, let's get back. Lecture's over."

Peter glanced at the empty sky a last time, then they turned down the hogback.

The third morning after they'd returned from the mountain, Peter awoke to the hardest frost he'd ever seen. Omar looked at the crystals hanging glistening in the brittle sun and said, "It's a black frost all right."

"It looks white to me," Peter said.

"White enough. It's gonna kill the grass and poplar and vine maple leaves and drive the sap down for the next four or five months. Farmers call it a black frost because it kills all vegetables left out, and they turn black and rot. Any day now that old snow line'll move right down through the trees to the riverbank."

"Then it'll be winter down here?"

"And that's a fact. Deer and elk'll be all around us."

By noon, frost-scorched leaves had loosed their grip and were drifting into the dying grass. A wind sprang up, and the following morning the trees were almost bare. For the first time, Peter could see the river from the cabin door. The sun came out, but the wind had a biting edge. In the shade, the frost did not leave.

"When it gets a little colder," Omar said, "we'll get us a deer."

"I thought you didn't believe in killing them," Peter said.

"Don't believe in slaughterin' 'em. But they're put here to use like everythin' else. Some years I get one, some I don't. This year, there being two of us, we need one."

Omar assumed part of the cooking again, but Peter prepared breakfast and lunch. Omar was always teaching him new ways to prepare food, especially how to make sourdough bread, biscuits, and several kinds of cookies. Peter came to believe, as Omar had said, that sourdough was the backbone of the settling of the West.

They kept the cabin door closed and a small fire going all day now. Peter took it upon himself to split wood and keep the wood box full. Between his cooking and wood-carrying he watched for a plane. A half-dozen times a day he dashed outside to look anxiously all about when he heard, or imagined he heard, some strange sound. Omar watched but said nothing.

A thin ice film made lacework along the river shore and blanketed the small, still pools. But out in the channel the current boomed along. Omar said it would continue all winter. "That water moves too fast to freeze."

Peter was glad for the extra clothing his mother had packed. But Omar insisted his jacket would not be warm enough when snow flew. He cut down one of his old ones to fit Peter. The boy was surprised at how handy the old man was with a needle and thread. "Out here you learn to do or do without," Omar said.

There came a morning when an inch of fresh snow covered the ground and weighed down the limbs of the big pine. "Now we'll get our deer," Omar announced.

They located the deer about a quarter of a mile from the cabin. They found fresh tracks in the snow and Omar said, "He's close around here." They followed the tracks in and out of the brush for about ten minutes, walking single file.

When Omar stopped suddenly, Peter looked around him, and there it was, about fifty yards off, in the act of nibbling buds from a bush.

"About a two-year-old," Omar murmured. He raised the rifle. At the sharp crack the buck dropped.

Omar drew the buck, fastened the front and rear legs together, and slung the carcass over his shoulder. Peter carried the rifle and they returned to the cabin.

They skinned out the deer under the lean-to in back. Bill came to watch, but the smell of blood and fresh meat annoyed him. He snorted and went off through the trees.

Omar carried it into the cabin. They spent most of the day cutting it up on the table. Peter was surprised at the change in his thinking between the kill and cutting up the meat. He'd felt bad at the killing. Now it was food. He was glad they had it.

Omar cut a lot of it into long strips to make jerky. He seasoned it, and spread it on a wire frame which they hung from the ceiling over the stove. The rest went into two white flour-sacks that they hung from a limb of the big pine by a long rope. "It'll freeze tonight," Omar explained. "But I hung it where it'll always be in the shade any time the sun shines. From now on, everything in the shade will stay frozen. This's our deep freeze till spring."

"Can't some animal get it?"

"It's hung too high for any animal to jump. And no climber's got brains enough to untie or gnaw through that rope to let it down. When we want a roast or steak, we'll take it in, saw off a piece with the handsaw, and hang the rest up again."

During the night Peter heard sounds outside. He peeked out the window. In the moonlight he saw two coyotes walking around the tree, looking up at the sacks. He tiptoed to Omar's room and awakened him. Together they peeked out at the animals. As they watched, one leaped upward a few feet short, then fell back. It crouched and leaped again and again.

"That's old Lonesome," Omar whispered. "He always had one ear that flopped down like a rag. I see he finally got a mate. They probably smelled that meat a quarter mile away."

"Aren't you going to shoot them?" Peter whispered.

"They ain't botherin' us any." Omar chuckled and went back to bed.

Peter checked the meat the first thing in the morning. The snow was cut up with doglike tracks, but the venison was untouched. When he returned, Omar had the fire going, and delicious warmth was spreading throughout the cabin along with a faint, mouth-watering aroma that was to last for days. The smell was of drying venison strips.

They ate breakfast in companionable silence, and afterward Peter asked, "How soon will this snow leave?"

"Might not leave altogether, or if it does, it'll be back soon. Winter's come to the canyon, Pete."

The words startled Peter and made him think of the time he'd been here. He'd continued to watch for the plane, but he hadn't kept track of the days. He looked at the calendar in the drawer and figured out the time he'd been here. This was the twenty-fourth day. Almost a month! Now it was winter, and a blanket of snow covered everything. Peter thought about that while they washed the dishes. Afterward, he put on his cap and coat and went out to his fire pile. From force of habit he glanced at the lowering sky. It was a snow sky. His fire pile was hidden under a blanket of snow. He began kicking it apart. He got an ax and chopped the sticks into stove-wood lengths. He carried them to the back and piled them in the lean-to with the rest of the wood. He was committed to staying in the canyon with Omar until the first jet boat came upriver next spring.

🌲🌲🌲🌲🌲🌲🌲 8 🌲🌲🌲🌲🌲🌲🌲

Now that he was reconciled to spending the winter in the canyon, and Omar and he got along so well, Peter no longer grieved for his home and parents. But they were always in the back of his mind, a warm presence to which he could turn when a sense of loneliness threatened to overwhelm him. For the most part there was so much to see and do that there was little time to be lonely.

Intermittent snow flurries gradually increased the depth to about four inches. The deer and elk herds followed the snow line down. They appeared regularly, and in great numbers, near the cabin and along the riverbank. Ice along the river thickened until Peter could walk on it near the shore. But out in the channel, the water went tearing along. The big rocks were crusted with ice from flying spray.

Omar fed Bill something from the table each morning and gave him a couple of nibbles of tobacco before the buck went off to join other deer for the day. At night he returned. Several times deer followed him, but they always refused to enter the shed.

The jerky was cured, cut into short lengths, packed in empty coffee cans, and stored in the pantry. Whenever Peter took a hike, he carried a couple of chunks in his pocket.

Even in this weather Omar stood out in the cold each night to whistle Solomon from the shed for a bit of food, and to hold their lengthy one-sided conversations. Winter had driven the mice underground. Now Omar fed the owl small pieces of thawed venison. He fixed a small sliding panel that covered the hole at the bottom of the door where the marten entered each night for his meal of sliced jerky. After Peter heard Marty eat, he'd get up and close the panel to keep out the cold. "Maybe it is sort of foolish," Omar admitted when Peter spoke of the cold that got in. "But wait till spring. You might change your mind."

They went often to check on the deer and elk herds. Peter learned all the verses Omar knew of "The Big Rock Candy Mountains" and "Down in the Valley." Sometimes one or the other of them made up a silly ditty as they hiked along, but usually they whistled. It was too cold to sing.

The sky remained clear, cold, and gunmetal blue with scarcely a cloud. The silence was complete except when they broke it.

Peter was not aware of any change in the weather until Omar squinted at the sky one day and an-

101

nounced, "We're gonna get a storm. Sky's changin'."

It had been so subtle and gradual that Peter hadn't noticed. The steely, deep blue was almost gone. It was being overlaid by a dull gray.

Omar studied it, then asked, "Pete, you ever been in a blizzard?" And when Peter shook his head, Omar said, "You're gonna be soon."

"We have a little snow at home," Peter said. "Sometimes it lasts a couple of days, but I've never seen a blizzard."

"We'd better be sure the wood box is full tonight. We won't put out the fire."

Peter awoke during the night to hear the wind slamming against the side of the cabin. Omar was up, filling the stove. He had removed one of the stove lids. Peter watched sleepily as the flames danced over his bony shoulders and chest and long arms.

With morning, their world was closed in to the rooms of the cabin. The windows were completely frosted over. Peter held his palm to the window to thaw a hole but could not see the river for the wind-driven snow. The big pine was blown clear of snow. Drifts were piling against the base of trees, rocks, or any other obstruction. The sacks of frozen venison swung in the wind.

"How long will this last?" Peter asked.

"No tellin' about a blizzard. I've known 'em to go for a week. Then again, I've seen 'em blow themselves out in a day or two. This bein' the first one, it may not last long."

Omar proved correct. The storm blew itself out. The following day was cold and clear. This, Omar predicted, would be the pattern of their winter with a couple of rip-snorting blizzards thrown in.

They were out almost every day, going somewhere or doing something to keep themselves occupied. Omar hounded Peter to keep his shoes well greased. He taught him a trick with an extra pair of socks. It helped keep his feet dry. You rolled them down over your shoe tops. This kept the snow out.

Peter was aware that Omar religiously checked off the calendar every night the last thing before turning in. But he carefully avoided keeping track of the dragging days. Omar mentioned it, and Peter explained, "When I count the days, they seem to go so slow, and I keep thinking about it. If I don't keep track, I don't think about it so much, and the time seems to go faster."

Omar smiled, "The old boilin' kettle, eh?"

"What's that?"

"Just a saying that the watched kettle never boils. It does, of course. But when you watch it, it always seems to take twice as long."

"I guess that's it," Peter said.

Peter was jerked out of a sound sleep by a series of thunderous explosions in the middle of the night. The cabin was lit, the door stood wide open. But most amazing of all, Omar stood outside the door in the snow wearing only his pants, shoes, and heavy underwear. He was firing the rifle into the night.

Peter tumbled out of his sleeping bag and ran to the door yelling, "What's wrong, Omar! What's happened?"

Omar grinned and waved the rifle. "Happy New Year!" he bellowed at the top of his lungs. "Happy New Year, Pete!"

"What?" Peter rubbed his eyes.

"Look at the calendar, Pete. Look at it."

Peter ran and got the calendar from the drawer. The last date crossed out was December 31.

"Come on, celebrate!" Omar yelled. "There's two shells left."

Peter ran out into the snow in his underwear and bare feet, grabbed the rifle, and blasted both shots at the stars. "Happy New Year, Omar!" he shouted. "Happy New Year!"

"Now let's get back inside before this Happy New Year turns into a wake," Omar said, shivering.

"What happened to Christmas?" Peter asked, pulling on his pants, shirt, and shoes. "What happened to Christmas, Omar?"

"Near as I can figure, that sleigh went over this canyon so blamed fast there just wasn't time to stop." Omar stood the rifle in the corner and explained, "Long as you didn't notice, I figured it'd be just as well to let it pass. Christmas can be a pretty rough time away from home. But New Year's, that's somethin' else. That says time's gettin' shorter. The old year's gone and the new one's started. We oughta celebrate."

They built up the fire again. Omar made coffee for

himself and chocolate for Peter. They opened a box of cookies that had been brought in last spring by jet boat and sat at the table and talked.

"Would you believe this's the first New Year I've celebrated since I came out here?" Omar said.

"The first in fifty years?" Peter asked, surprised.

"That's right. Man can't have a party alone. I wouldn't have celebrated this one but for you."

"Then I'm glad I'm here," Peter said and meant it.

"Me, too. What'd you be doin' if you was home, Pete?"

Peter leaned his elbows on the table and smiled thoughtfully. "We'd probably have a little party at home with some friends. Mother and Dad aren't much for nightclubbing. We'd sit around and play some silly games and wait for midnight, then all go out on the porch and look down on a million lights of the city and listen to all the whistles and bells and sirens and things."

"Last one I remember celebratin' I was at a box social at a little wooden schoolhouse."

"What's a box social?"

"That's where the women fix up fancy boxes of eats and they're auctioned off. Whatever box you win, you get to eat with the lady that fixed it. I remember somebody set off a string of firecrackers about six feet long. Just out of town some fool put a full box of dynamite on a stump and shot into it with a rifle. Busted windows in a house almost a quarter mile away."

They talked and drank coffee and chocolate and ate

the box of cookies. Finally Omar yawned. "Gonna be mornin' before we know it." He replenished the fire and banked it.

Peter crawled into his sleeping bag again and looked up as Omar prepared to blow out the light. "I'll bet this was the queerest New Year's party in a hundred miles," he said.

"I'll bet," Omar agreed.

"And the best," Peter said, smiling.

Omar nodded. "Don't take lots of people to make a good party. Just the right ones. Night." He blew out the light and went into his room.

Peter snuggled deep into his sleeping bag. Silence settled over the cabin.

The new year was already two hours old.

9

They got their first rip-snorter of a blizzard the middle of January.

The deer and elk herds disappeared. Omar said they were out of the storm in the thick brush or against protective banks.

Peter ventured outside only to get wood. The driving wind cut the heat from his body the few minutes he was out. It left him chilled to the bone.

Omar fed Bill and Solomon, who both stayed in the shed. He brought in a sack of frozen venison and cut three big steaks. "No sense gettin' into this storm every day for a piece," he explained. "These'll hold us three or four days. Maybe in that time the storm'll be over."

Snow swirled across the earth. Wind whistled at the corners of the cabin. But inside, the stove threw out heat and the cabin was warm and comfortable. Watching the storm became monotonous, and Peter wandered about the room.

The lamp was lit even in the middle of the day. Omar sat at the table laboriously mending a torn shirt.

He said, without looking up, "This's the hardest part of livin' alone out here, being cooped up by a blizzard. If you can take this, you can make it all right. Lots of men find they can't. Some've gone temporarily crazy. Cabin fever they call it. Now this winter, I've got it soft, you bein' with me and all. And that's a fact."

"How did you manage in the past?"

Omar bit off the thread and inspected the patched pocket. "Secret's in keepin' busy at something. Spring, summer, and fall's no problem. You can always be outside and find a hundred things to think about and do. Winter's somethin' else. I think up something different to cook, or mend a shirt, or I read that pile of newspapers and old magazines again. Maybe I'll read the same article or story four or five times. Can't tell, I mighta missed something the first couple of times," he said. "Seein' as you don't sew and have got nothin' to make, you'd better head for that pile of magazines. Now that I got this shirt patched I'm gonna make a gold-dust poke outa that deer hide." He got out the hide and began to cut and sew.

Peter read. The wind howled. The snow piled higher on the windowsill. The frost was a quarter-inch thick on the glass. Dark came early. Peter loaded the wood box.

Omar finished his poke and poured the gold dust into it.

They ate supper. Omar went out and fed Bill a couple of leftover biscuits. He took an extra helping of fresh venison cubes to Solomon.

108

"You're not going to leave the sliding door open for Marty tonight?" Peter asked.

"Of course. I worked with him for months before I got him to come in like he does now."

"But it'll let in a lot of cold."

"Not much. That hole's not so big, and the wind's hittin' the other side of the cabin. Anyway, Marty's like a neighbor that drops in daily for a cup of coffee. He helps break the monotony. If we lock him out, he might never come back. You can close the trap door as soon as you hear him leave."

Peter didn't argue. But he reminded himself that he'd almost forgotten Omar was a little queer.

They went to bed early. Omar didn't bank the fire but stoked it with wood and closed the drafts. Peter lay listening to the dismal sound of the wind and thinking of the cold air funneling through the hole at the bottom of the door. Finally he heard the rattling of the tin pan.

He turned his head and in the faint light thrown by the stove's fire box, he made out the shape of the marten. He finished in a few minutes and vanished. Peter got up and dropped the slide door.

The second day was a repetition of the first. It seemed to Peter he carried wood most of the day, and when he wasn't carrying, he was stuffing the stove. Omar announced that Bill hadn't stirred from his bed or Solomon from his crossbeam. "They're smart. Both getting in plenty of bunk time when there's nothing else they can do. Think I'll do the same." He rolled into bed and slept all afternoon. Peter returned to the old magazines.

The third day was the same. The wind blew as if it would never stop. The snow swirled as if it always had and always would. Again, Omar took bunk time, grumbling, "It's a real sin, a man sleepin' so long, and that's a fact." Peter carried wood, kept the fire, and thumbed through the magazines and papers.

Peter didn't hear Omar stoke the fire during the night. When he awoke, something was different. There was no wind. He crawled from the sleeping bag, went to the door, and opened it. There was not a sound. Not a flake of snow was falling. He could see all the way to the riverbank. The trees stood stark and motionless, their limbs blown bare of snow. The sacks of venison hung straight down from the pine limb. A short distance off, a half-dozen cow elk and a bull were industriously pawing down through a foot of light snow to get at the grass clumps. It was a still, white, frigid, beautiful world.

Peter slammed the door and ran to Omar's room, "The storm's over!" he yelled. "Omar, the storm's over."

Omar sat up, yawned hugely, and scratched his head, "Yellin' loud enough to wake the dead," he grumbled.

"But it's over. The storm's over."

"Knew that when I stoked the fire at two o'clock."

"Why didn't you wake me?"

110

"You was havin' a good snooze. Knew it'd still be over this morning."

They celebrated with pancakes, maple syrup, and two slices each of a small can of ham that Omar opened for this special occasion.

After breakfast Omar said, "What say we take a hike, get the kinks outa our legs and see how everythin' made out?"

"What things?" Peter asked.

"The animals, of course," Omar said. "Ranchers got cattle, sheep, horses, and such to look after. I've got deer and elk."

Peter piled on all the clothing he could because Omar explained, "Now's the most dangerous time of all. The still cold eats into a man and he begins to freeze without knowin' it."

Although the snow was almost a foot deep, walking was easy because it was powdery dry and light. Bill came from the shed and trotted up to Omar expectantly. Omar dug a plug of tobacco from his pocket, twisted off a piece, and gave it to him. Omar slapped him on the rump, "Now beat it. Go find yourself something to eat like the other deer." Bill followed a few steps. Then, since no more tobacco was forthcoming, he turned off into the trees.

Omar began to whistle "The Big Rock Candy Mountains." In the winter stillness, the sound carried and carried.

They found the first band of elk almost immediately.

111

The animals stopped pawing and stared at them as they passed. Deer and elk bands were scattered all through this low area as thick as cattle. The elk cows stayed mostly together in small groups, the bulls by themselves. The deer were scattered out singly, in pairs, and sometimes in small mixed groups.

Omar moved slowly. He never walked straight toward an animal or a group. He angled off, seeming to be going away, but actually approaching. When they came too near, the animals moved off, never letting them approach beyond a distance which they seemed to set.

Peter and Omar made a great circle up through the timber and back to the river. The river ice had crept out twenty or thirty feet into the channel. Close to shore it was thick enough to hold their combined weight. They came to the jutting shoulder of rock that Peter had followed Bill around after the plane crash.

They stopped and Omar said, "We might as well head back. There's no use goin' further."

They were turning to leave when a deer's head appeared out in the current, swimming around the rock. She was swimming frantically across the current, making for the ice. Her nostrils were flared, her eyes big and frightened. She made the ice and tried to climb out. The thin outer crust broke and the current sucked her back. She made the ice a second time, almost in front of them. She got her slender forelegs on top and hung there.

Omar said, "She's worn out. She'll never make it."

He handed Peter the rifle and started across the ice. He was still ten feet away when the ice began to crack. Omar dropped flat, distributing his weight. He wriggled toward the doe. She hung there, seeming to know that if she slipped back into the river again, she'd drown.

Omar inched forward carefully. Finally he reached out a big hand, grasped the loose skin of her neck, and hauled her, kicking feebly, out on the ice. She struggled a little, then lay still.

Peter laid the rifle against a rock and went out as far as he dared. Omar crawled back, shoving the deer across the ice ahead of him. Peter carried her to the bank and put her down. She collapsed and lay shivering.

Omar bent over, examining her. "No broken legs," he announced. "She could have been swimmin' quite a while fightin' that current."

"What was she doing swimming in that icy water?"

"Maybe trying to get away from some predator. Or she could have been out on the ice and broke through. There's no tellin'. But in her condition she'll die here in this cold. We've got to get her to the cabin where we can dry her off and get her warm." He peeled off his heavy jacket, wrapped it about the shivering animal, and gathered her up in his arms.

She was young and not too heavy. Omar carried her about a hundred yards before he had to put her down to rest. He stood panting, holding a hand to his chest, "Guess I ain't so young." He shook his head.

Peter handed him the rifle, "I'll carry her a ways. Take your jacket off her and we'll use mine."

"You can carry her," Omar said, "but your jacket's too small. It's got to be mine."

She didn't struggle or kick when Peter picked her up. But through the foot-deep snow he managed only about fifty yards when he had to put her down.

Omar handed him the rifle. "My turn."

So they made their way to the cabin. But it was slow going. Peter didn't know how long it took, but he was tired. He could see that Omar was near exhaustion and chilled to the bone. His lips were blue with cold.

They put the deer on the floor in front of the stove. Omar sat down. He was shivering as much as the doe, and he kept rubbing a hand over his chest. There was a white rim about his mouth. He shook his head, muttering, "That's about all I can take. 'Bout all I can take."

Peter shook up the fire, stuffed the stove with wood, and opened the drafts wide for quick heat. He pulled off Omar's shirt and wrapped a blanket around him. Then he got a couple of sacks from the pantry and began to wipe the deer dry. Omar slumped in the chair and watched. After a few minutes, Omar knelt stiffly beside Peter to help.

The doe lay stretched full-length, too exhausted to lift her head. They dried her and turned her. Omar showed Peter how to massage her muscles. They worked for an hour. Heat spread through the room. The doe quit shivering, but she didn't move.

Finally Omar sat back and studied her. "She needs

114

somethin' to give her a lift or we're gonna lose her."
He went into the pantry and returned with a bottle.
"Just about enough left for a couple of good shots," he
announced. "You hold up her head, Pete."

Omar poured a tablespoonful of liquor. Peter held
the doe's head. Omar pried her mouth open and
poured the liquor down. He held her mouth shut until
she swallowed. He gave her two more tablespoonsful,
and the bottle was empty.

They sat and waited. The doe lay motionless.
Lunchtime came.

Peter made sandwiches with the can of ham left
over from breakfast, coffee for Omar, and chocolate
for himself. They ate and watched the deer.

"She seems to look a little brighter, don't you
think?" Peter asked.

"I think, maybe." Omar had eaten very little. He
kept rubbing his chest.

"Is anything wrong?" Peter asked.

"I didn't do somethin' in here any good with all that
carryin' and crawlin' around on the ice. Think I'll turn
in for a little while. Call me if she starts to move." He
rose and went into the bedroom.

Peter cleaned up the dishes, filled the stove again,
and sat down to watch the deer. Her fur was dry now
and she seemed to be resting. Those big, liquid eyes
were open, watching him. But she didn't move.

Finally Peter went to the pile of dog-eared magazines, found a story he'd passed over before, and began
to read it. He was about halfway through when the

deer raised her head, then slowly gathered first one leg and then another under her.

Peter ran to the bedroom and said, "Omar, the deer's about to get up."

Omar came heavily into the kitchen. "You're right. We don't want her gettin' up in here. She'll be scared and'll run wild and tear up the place. Get the door open, then pick her up and carry her outside. She's ready to be turned loose."

Peter opened the door. But when he returned to pick up the doe, she lunged unsteadily to her feet.

"Get behind her and shove her out the door," Omar said. "Quick! Before she gets her balance."

Peter turned her, got both hands on her rump, and propelled her, sliding and slipping, across the floor and out the door. She stood a minute, spraddle-legged and uncertain. Then she started to walk off through the snow. After a couple dozen steps she began to trot. The last Peter saw of her, she was trotting steadily off through the trees. He closed the door.

"Our good deed for the day," Omar said, and returned to the bedroom.

10

Peter awoke to a cold room. The fire was out. Omar hadn't replenished it during the night. He got the fire going, then looked in on Omar. He lay on his back, awake. His leathery cheeks were flushed, his voice husky. He sounded very tired. "Just didn't have the energy to get up and stoke the fire, and that's a mortal fact," he said.

"I've got it going. The room'll be warm soon. You want to get up then?"

"I'll think about it." Omar moved his long legs under the blanket. "Never felt so downright beat in my whole life before."

"Do you hurt any place special?"

"Chest feels like somebody stuck a hot iron into it every time I cough. Tired mostly, though. Just tired."

"You shouldn't have taken off your coat and put it around the deer. It was cold and you got a chill. You should have let me carry her more, even if it would have taken longer."

"Could be part of it," Omar agreed. "Could be

crawlin' around on the ice, too. And seventy-some years could be a big part of it."

"I'll get breakfast right away," Peter said. "Do you want anything special?"

Omar shook his head. "Cup of coffee, maybe. And there's a couple cans of tomato juice on the shelf in the pantry. Glass of that might go good."

When he finally came to breakfast, Omar drank a cup of coffee, scarcely touched the tomato juice, and returned to bed. "Maybe tonight I'll feel more like it. You might cut us a steak and let it thaw. Add an extra little chunk for Solomon."

Peter brought in one of the sacks, cut a steak for each of them, and a piece for the owl. He put it on top of the oven to thaw. The rest of the morning Peter spent puttering about the cabin.

Bill came from the shed and stopped in front of the cabin as though waiting for Omar to appear. Finally, he went off among the trees.

Peter peeked into the bedroom, but Omar seemed to be sleeping. At lunchtime Omar was awake, and Peter asked what he'd like to eat.

"Not hungry, Pete. Just not hungry. I'd sure like a cold drink of water, though."

Peter got it and felt Omar's forehead. It was hot. "You've got a fever. Is there any medicine here?"

Omar shook his head. "Don't think so. Been years since I took any. Might look around those shelves in the pantry."

Peter found an empty aspirin bottle and another

bottle that had once contained a liquid. But it had dried up. He told Omar and asked, "What about a first-aid kit? You should have a first-aid kit out here."

"There's one in the top drawer of the dresser. But all it's got is bandages and tape and a couple splints. Things for cuts and broken bones. No medicine. Quit keepin' that years ago. I never got sick, and it spoiled." He smiled faintly. "You'll have to take over the cookin' and things till I get back on my feet."

"I will."

"You're gettin' to be a pretty fair cook, and that's the truth," Omar murmured. He seemed to sleep again.

That night Peter prepared the steak as Omar had taught him. He turned it quickly on either side, searing it to hold the juices. He finished it rare, the way Omar liked it. He made sourdough biscuits and gravy to pour over them, and opened a can of Omar's favorite peaches.

Omar came into the kitchen, a blanket wrapped about him. He sat at the table and said, "Looks good, Pete. Mighty good." He ate only a few bites of steak and half a biscuit and pushed his plate away. "Give the rest to Marty tonight."

Omar pulled his chair close to the stove and sat hunched up, soaking in the heat. In spite of the rest he'd had, he still looked tired. His bony shoulders were stooped, his gray eyes dull. His normally brown skin was pale beneath the stubble. For the first time his big, bony frame looked frail to Peter.

A wave of apprehension went through him and he

119

asked, "Can I get you anything, Omar? Anything at all?"

Omar shook his head, "Not a thing, Pete." He roused after a few minutes and asked, "You fed Solomon yet?"

"No," Peter said, "I can't call him from the shed like you can."

Omar didn't answer immediately. Finally he said, "Just not up to gettin' dressed and standin' out there in the cold tonight."

Peter had cleared the table and finished washing the dishes when he heard the hollow *whoo-whoo-ooo* from the pine tree. Solomon was tired of waiting and was calling Omar.

Omar turned his head and looked toward the door. He smiled faintly.

Peter slipped into his coat and put on his cap. "I'll feed him." He took the leather glove, got the raw meat for the owl, and went outside.

Peter walked to the spot where Omar usually stood, pulled on the glove, and held the piece of meat at arm's length. He didn't try to mimic Solomon's call because he knew he couldn't. He held his arm out and looked up at the black blob of the owl. It was bright moonlight and he saw Solomon plainly. The owl stared down at him. Peter guessed he was waiting for Omar's soft call. His arm began to ache. He was about ready to drop the meat in the snow when Solomon shot off the branch. He circled low over Peter once and came back. For an instant he seemed to hesitate at Peter's fingertips, then he was gone, and so was the piece of meat. Solomon sailed silently back to the limb.

Peter held out the second piece. Again he waited until his arm was getting tired before Solomon ghosted from the limb and took the meat.

Peter returned to the cabin. Omar glanced up. "Did he take it?"

"Yes."

"Thanks, Pete." Omar rose heavily. "Guess I'll go back to bed. Seems I ought to get enough rest pretty soon."

Omar didn't get up for breakfast, and Peter took it in to him. He drank a little coffee and waved the rest away. "It's just not in me to eat, Pete," he said.

The weather changed. A brittle sun came out, and the temperature rose. The snow began to thaw in the sun during the daylight hours. At night it froze. It continued to thaw and freeze the next couple of days.

Omar got no better. He didn't leave the bed. Several times Peter had seen him spit up blood. He looked more frail than ever. Peter was worried, then frightened. He prepared every dish he knew to try to tempt Omar's appetite, but it was no use.

"I think I can eat," Omar murmured, "then I can't. Don't worry about it."

"I wish we had some medicine I could give you. I wish I could do something."

"You're doin' fine." He squeezed Peter's hand. "I'm

sorry you can't be home, but I'm real glad you're here. It's no fun being sick alone, and that's a fact. I've worried about that some the past couple years."

Peter squeezed the bony fingers. A lump swelled in his throat, and his eyes stung. "I'm glad I'm here, Omar."

Omar wanted to talk. Peter suggested he be quiet and conserve his strength. Omar shook his head, "Won't matter, Pete. I know." His eyes were very bright. His breathing was a noisy, labored sound in the room. Peter wasn't sure he was rational. Some of the things he said made little sense.

"Like I told you. The secret to livin' alone out here is to keep busy. Makes no difference if what you do is important or not. Make it important to you. And maybe if you look real hard, you'll find it is." He was silent a moment. Peter waited, not knowing what to say. Omar's big fingers knotted and unknotted on the quilt. "Plenty of food here. But man has to be careful. Don't waste it. Most important thing of all is the calendar. Only way you got of keepin' track of time. Always cross off each day the last thing at night. In the spring I watch for the river to start risin'. May or June, dependin' on how the snow pack melts. Jet boats'll be comin' up as soon as the water covers the big rocks. They'll stop right here, too."

"We can both go out then," Peter said gently.

Omar looked at him a long moment. Then he murmured, "Yeah, sure. Sure. We'll both go out."

A few minutes later, he seemed to go to sleep. Peter

stood listening to the heavy breathing and thinking about the old man. Then he tiptoed from the room.

That evening when Peter took supper in, Omar looked at the food he'd worked so hard to make inviting and shook his head. "You've got to eat," Peter said. "You've got to get your strength back. You've lost weight, Omar. You've got to try."

"Maybe later, Pete." Omar moved his hands over the covers. "I been thinkin', Pete. Surprisin' how much thinkin' a man can do when he can't get about."

"What have you been thinking about, Omar?"

Omar straightened his legs. "Mostly about you and me and you comin' here. That was a mighty big thing to me, Pete. Kinda like havin' company when you ain't had any for fifty years. Put the food away, Pete. Don't sit there holdin' it."

Peter put the food in the warming oven and returned to the bedroom. Omar was staring thoughtfully at the ceiling. "Would you like a drink?" Peter asked.

Omar shook his head. He sighed noisily and said, "You once asked me about that grave out there, and I snapped you off short. I shouldn't have done that."

"I was just curious," Peter said. "It was none of my business. I shouldn't have asked." Suddenly he didn't want to know.

Omar continued as if he hadn't heard, "You got every right to know, Pete. You bein' here with me and all, taking care of me now. No man could ask for a better partner, and that's a fact. I want you to know how it was."

123

Peter sat on the edge of the chair. He could see Omar's mind slipping back through the years. Finally the old man said, "It was a long time ago, fifty years ago. I remember plain as yesterday—always could." He was quiet, breathing heavily.

"I was pretty young, twenty-four, no twenty-five. I was a guide, took parties out in the wilds huntin' and fishin'. I'd been at it about a year when this party of six men hired me for an elk-huntin' trip. They were all big, successful businessmen. I was years younger than the youngest of them. We packed into this country about seventy miles. There was no jet boats them days. We got caught in an early blizzard, one of the worst I've ever known. The second night, our horses stampeded, a cougar or somethin'. We never saw hide nor hair of 'em again.

"We figured the blizzard would blow itself out in a day or two, it bein' the first of the winter. So we waited. One of the party took sick, feller named Edward Dennis. Don't know what he had, but he got worse and worse. We stuck it out for a week. Most of our grub was gone. It was bitter cold. It didn't look like the blizzard would ever end. We had to get out or stay and freeze or starve to death." Omar paused. His breathing was painful.

Peter said, "Tell me tomorrow. Rest now, Omar."

"Those five businessmen decided to pull out and leave the sick man," Omar said. "When they told me, I refused. I wanted to improvise a stretcher and carry him with us. The one who'd appointed himself spokesman said no, that we'd be lucky to get out as it was. The sick man would only slow us down, and we'd all die. There was no sense six men dyin' to save one that was goin' to die anyway. It did look like Dennis wouldn't make it. But I still refused. Then this feller pointed his rifle at me and threatened to kill me if I didn't guide them out. Even Dennis told me to leave him. So we did."

Omar was looking at Peter. But the boy felt those gray eyes were not seeing him.

"I gave Dennis half my blankets, scrounged up a couple handfuls of raisins and two little pieces of chocolate. The others insisted on taking the tent, so I made Dennis a lean-to out of limbs and brush, piled a lot of firewood close at hand so he could reach it, left him his rifle and all the matches I had.

"The second day after we left Dennis, the storm broke. The fourth mornin', we stumbled into a trapper's shack. The trapper had grub, and he knew the way out. Those five hired him to take them the rest of the way, and I headed back for Edward Dennis." Omar stopped, his breathing shallow.

"You're tired," Peter said. "Let it go for now."

Omar shook his head, "Be all right in a minute." When he resumed, he said, "Man who held the rifle on me, who was the leader of those five men, was James T. Sutton, Senior."

"The head of the logging company that wants to cut this timber?" Peter asked.

"Father of the one headin' it now. Funny, huh?"

"Yes," Peter said. "Did you find Edward Dennis?"

Omar shook his head. "When I got back to the lean-to he was gone, and there was his tracks in the snow. I followed 'em and found him within half a mile of here, dead. He'd managed to travel more'n six miles. I couldn't take him out, so I brought him down here and buried him. He'd seen this spot and loved it.

"It wasn't hard to figure out most of what had happened. When the storm ended, he tried to walk out. He didn't know which way to go. The storm had filled in our tracks. He took the easiest route, which was downhill. Only thing I couldn't figure was whether he got better after we left, or wasn't as sick as we all thought. Or whether he made one last-ditch effort in a delirium. I do know for a fact that since he hiked as far as he did, we could have taken him out with us."

"It wasn't your fault," Peter said with great relief. "You couldn't know the storm would quit, or that he'd get better, or that he could make that last big effort. You had five other people that you were responsible for. And they even threatened you."

Omar moved his legs restlessly. "Told myself that a thousand times, Pete. It's no excuse. The unwritten law of mountain men is that when one is in trouble, it's better to lose your own life tryin' to help him than to prove a coward."

"But you were only twenty-five and had been guiding just a year," Peter pointed out. "They were much older and five to one."

"No excuse. I was a coward."

126

"But Sutton threatened to shoot you."

"That was bluff. He didn't dare. I was the guide, the only one that knew the way out. I let 'em bluff me, Pete. If I'd stood fast and demanded that they take Dennis along, they'd have had to. But I didn't. Old Jim Sutton was big and confident and so sure of himself." Omar made small motions with his hands. "I just couldn't stand against him then. That's all."

"That doesn't mean you killed Dennis," Peter insisted. "He'd surely have died on the way back. You said it took four days to reach that trapper's cabin. After the storm was over, he only hiked about six miles and died of exposure. Don't you see, he could never have stood it for four days."

"With help I think he'd have made it, Pete. Anyway, he'd have had a chance. I robbed him of that chance. I should have stood fast. Man should always fight for what he believes in. Then if you lose, you've got nothin' to be ashamed of. You got to try."

Peter said nothing for a moment, and Omar's breathing was noisy and labored.

Finally Peter asked, "Is that why you came out here to live?"

"Partly." Omar smoothed the cover. "When I got back, Jim Sutton had already spread his version of the story. That Edward Dennis had died and that I made the decision to leave him there. I told what really happened. But Sutton's friends stuck with him. They were all respected men. I was a twenty-five-year-old nobody, who'd panicked the first time he got into trouble. As a guide, I was ruined. Guidin' was all I knew, or wanted to know. I loved this country, so I came back here to live." He sighed tiredly, "Sort of figured I owed it to Dennis. I'd run out on him once."

Peter sat there. There didn't seem to be anything to say.

Omar finally said, "Maybe I could eat a little now, Pete."

He ate almost everything Peter had put into the warming oven. "That was mighty good," he announced. "You're gettin' to be quite a cook, and that's the truth. I think I feel a little better. I've got a feelin' I'm gonna get a good night's sleep."

Peter told him good night, fixed Marty's tin plate of jerky shavings, banked the fire, and crawled into his sleeping bag. He felt better than he had for days. Omar had eaten a good supper, and the mystery of the grave was cleared up. He heard Marty rattle his pan as he ate. He waited a few minutes, then got up and closed the trap door. Lonesome and his mate yap-yapped far up in the hills. Solomon called *whoo-whoo-ooo* from the pine tree. The weather had definitely turned warmer. He could sleep straight through without refilling the stove.

When Peter awoke, it was full daylight and the room was cold. He dressed hurriedly, rekindled the fire, and cracked the damper open for quick heat. He peeked in at Omar. He was sleeping quietly, one arm bent over his eyes to shut out the morning light. Peter smiled and closed the door. He tiptoed about the kitchen, setting the table and preparing breakfast. When it was ready, he went to wake Omar. Omar hadn't moved. Peter said quietly, "Omar, do you want breakfast now?"

Omar didn't answer.

Peter said gently again, "Omar, wake up, breakfast's ready." Then he became aware of the complete silence in the room. He reached out and lifted Omar's arm from across his eyes. A great shock went rolling through him and he said softly, "Omar! Oh, Omar!"

Omar Pickett was dead.

Peter returned to the kitchen and sat down at the table. He began to shake. He gripped the edges of the table. The spasm passed, but he continued to sit there. He tried not to think. The coffeepot boiled over, and he pulled it off the stove.

He sat there a long time. The fire went down, and the stove had become cold when he finally began to think where he should bury Omar. There was only one place. He put on his cap and coat, went around to the lean-to, got the pick and shovel, and headed up to Edward Dennis's grave.

The earth was flint-hard. Peter had to pick down through a foot of frozen earth to reach soft soil.

Bill came up. He shook his horns and stamped his feet and started for Peter. Peter picked up a rock and bounced it off the deer's ribs. He yelled angrily, "Get out of here. Go on, beat it!"

Bill disappeared into the trees and didn't come back.

It was noon when he finally finished.

Omar was too heavy to carry. He found a couple of poles and some loose boards in the shed. He chopped the ends of the poles into crude sled runners and nailed the boards across them. He wrapped Omar in a blanket and got him onto the sled easier than he'd thought. Omar had lost a lot of weight. Pulling the sled was the hardest of all.

The sun was gone. The stars were out, and the chill of evening was biting into him when he finished. He stood over Omar's grave thinking, "I should say something." He'd felt closer to Omar than any man he'd ever known, his own father even. He'd come to love the crusty, odd old man. Finally he said, "I'm sorry, Omar. You'll never know how sorry." Then he walked away.

At the cabin he built up the fire. He remembered he'd eaten nothing all day. He was hungry, but the thought of preparing a meal was distasteful. He found a piece of bread and a chunk of cold venison and sat at the table and began to eat it. Warmth began to spread through the room. He remembered the calendar, got it, and crossed off the date.

Peter had just finished the bread and meat when he heard the familiar *whoo-whoo-ooo* from the pine tree. Solomon was tired of waiting and was calling for Omar to come feed him. Peter put his head down on the table and began to cry.

130

🌲🌲🌲🌲🌲🌲🌲 11 🌲🌲🌲🌲🌲🌲🌲

The fire burned low. The night's chill crept into the cabin. Solomon stopped calling from the pine tree. Some time later, Peter heard the faint scratching at the door. Marty was trying to get in for his jerky supper, but the hole was closed by the sliding door. Peter felt too discouraged and low in spitit to do anything about it. Marty finally left. He rebuilt the fire, banked it, and crawled into his sleeping bag.

Sleep would not come. He lay listening to the soft sounds he'd heard so often: the scrape of a limb against the log wall, the murmur of the breeze through the pines, and the creak and snapping of wood with the changing temperature. They all reminded him that now he was alone in a virgin wilderness. And he would remain alone until the first jet boat battled its way upriver next spring.

Later he heard Marty scratching at the door. The excited yapping of a pair of coyotes drifted on the stillness. Lonesome and his mate were running hot on some animal's trail. Solomon returned to the pine and began calling again. Peter was thinking what a lonely sound that was when he drifted off to sleep.

Peter felt no better in the morning. All he wanted to do was sit and think how much he missed Omar and how alone he felt. He made himself work. He cleaned up Omar's room, made the bed, and put everything in its place. Then he completely cleaned the cabin, emptied the stove's ashes, and took inventory of his food. There was more than enough to last. Besides the canned and packaged food there were twenty-five or thirty pounds of jerky and a two-pound can of Star plug tobacco for Bill.

In the following days, Peter drove himself, knowing that only by keeping busy could he keep from thinking about Omar and himself. He split enough wood to last for several weeks, then went out with the saw, cut down a couple of small trees, bucked them up, and dragged them in. But the depression stayed. He caught himself going into Omar's room at odd times to ask how he felt, or to see what he wanted for lunch. Several times when he walked into the cabin and didn't see Omar, he looked about expectantly. Then that sick feeling returned. He refused to think ahead to the next day, or even the next hour. He worked so that he was dead tired at night. Then he'd sleep.

He often heard Marty and Solomon, but so great was his grief and depression that he hadn't the heart to do anything about them. Bill usually came from the shed in the morning, or Peter would see him returning

132

from the timber in the late afternoon. The deer looked at him and shook his antlers, but Peter ignored him.

Sunk in his own misery, Peter didn't notice that something finally changed. Then he realized that for several nights Marty hadn't scratched at the door. He sliced jerky, put out the pan, and left the sliding door open. Marty didn't come. He couldn't remember when he'd last heard Solomon.

Peter went to the shed and verified that the owl was still there, high on his perch on the ridge pole. He thought, "If he comes to the pine again and calls, I'll go out and feed him."

As for Bill, the deer ignored Peter. Peter took a plug of tobacco out and tossed it into the grass near him. He had no desire to go up to the deer and hand-feed him. But Bill walked off and did not see the tobacco. Peter retrieved it and returned it to the can. He felt sorry about the three animals. They were Omar's pets. There was nothing he could do about it now. He guessed it was just as well that they'd gone wild again and were foraging.

But grief cannot last forever. By the end of a week Peter was ready for another hike to look around.

The weather had been holding well, thawing in the sun and freezing at night. Gradually, the snow around the cabin melted, leaving only small patches in the shade. The snow line was retreating, and the herds of deer and elk followed.

After breakfast Peter loaded up the rifle, stuffed a

133

couple of chunks of jerky into his pocket, and was off. He made a big circle, up to the snow line, then back down to the river and the cabin. It was noon. He'd eaten both chunks of jerky and was ravenously hungry. He felt better than he had in days. It was strange, but out there, walking around among the deer and elk, following the same trails Omar and he had taken many times had given him the feeling that Omar was somehow near.

He went out somewhere every day after that. There was something different or new on almost every hike. He was careful on these jaunts to avoid Omar's grave. But once he forgot and, returning, walked straight onto it. He stood there, and a great loss came over him. It took a full day to shake the feeling.

Omar had trained him well. Not once on a hike did Peter encounter a problem with any animal. The deer and elk noted his presence, but they were getting used to seeing him and hearing his soft whistle or singing. He moved quietly, slowly, as Omar had taught him. He came to recognize certain individuals, the two bulls Omar and he had watched fighting were often close together and seemed companionable now. There was the little band of five cows with three calves that hung out together. There was a beautiful mule buck whose perfection was ruined by one broken horn, who invariably dashed off fifty or a hundred feet, then whirled to stare at him. Peter did not see Bill on these hikes, and he wondered where the buck hung out. He caught glimpses of Lonesome and his mate several times, and once he saw where they'd caught and eaten a rabbit.

The only trouble he encountered was of his own making. He was hiking upriver one afternoon and came to the big shoulder of rock that thrust into the river. He stood there thinking of the plane wreck and Frank Eldridge. He hadn't been back since the day Bill led him out of the little canyon. On impulse he wanted to see the canyon, the plane, and Frank's grave again.

The pale winter sun and the current had cut the ice back until it extended only a few feet from the bank. He tested it close to shore, and it held his weight. He edged out, rounded the rock, and was again in the small canyon.

The plane, lying under the two pine trees, was covered with snow. It looked as though it had been there for years. He rummaged through the broken interior in the hope that Omar and he had missed something. There was nothing of value. The snow had thawed from Frank's grave. It looked exactly as it had the day they'd mounded the rocks over it. He stayed but a little while.

Rounding the shoulder of rock on the return, he stepped too far out on the ice. It broke, and he went through waist deep into the freezing water. He tried to climb out, but the ice kept breaking and dropping him back into the river. Finally, with the butt of the rifle he smashed the ice ahead of him and waded ashore. By the time he reached the cabin, his clothing was freezing. He didn't go back again.

This was the state of things when the next storm

moved off the high peaks and engulfed the gorge. The sun disappeared behind the cloud bank which blotted out the sky and turned the day gray. The deer and elk knew. They were already down along the river. The storm closed down over the mountains like a misty curtain. The first big flakes began to fall. Peter filled the wood box and piled several armloads on the floor near the stove.

Daylight faded early. Through the thick-falling snow Peter barely made out the shed. This was no wind-howling blizzard. The big, fat flakes floated silently down, gradually bending the trees with their weight. By night, when Peter went to bed, it was already four inches deep and falling steadily.

Peter replenished the fire once during the night. He looked out the window. It was snowing quietly. By morning there was almost a foot, and it was still coming.

It snowed all day, that night, and the next day. When it finally slacked off and quit, it was just above Peter's knees. He'd had three days inside the cabin, walking from window to window to look out. He'd read and reread everything that might faintly interest him in the old magazines and papers until he knew them by heart. There was not an animal about. No bird made a sound. It was a white, dead, silent world. He wished the wind would blow. He checked his food supply again. He rummaged through Omar's few belongings, looking for anything of interest. He cleaned the rifle a second, then a third time. He remembered

Omar got plenty of bunk time during the storm. He turned in and slept all afternoon. Then he was awake all night, tossing and turning. He waited for any sound to break the stillness. He hadn't heard Lonesome and his mate since the storm began. He guessed they'd left for other parts. The night silence was most oppressive of all.

He couldn't stand the monotony of nothing to do another twenty-four hours. This was what made lonely prospectors and trappers get cabin fever, Omar had said. He realized he hadn't spoken a word aloud for days. Tomorrow, he told himself, regardless of the deep snow and cold, he was going for a hike.

Peter was up early, made breakfast, and prepared for his hike. He put on an extra pair of socks, a second sweater over the first, his heavy jacket, cap, and a pair of Omar's mittens. He loaded the rifle and stuffed extra shells into his pocket, with several chunks of jerky. He headed out whistling "Down in the Valley." He was surprised how cheerful the notes sounded in the stillness.

The snow had formed a crust. He broke through at every step.

Deer and elk were scattered through this low land. The deer browsed on last summer's tender growth of brush, while the elk pawed through the snow to get at the dead grass and low ground cover. The deer were further up the slope than he'd expected. Then he understood why. They'd eaten so much of the tender browse along the river that now they were forced higher. The snow crust was thicker, and it was harder for the deer to get about. They made little effort to move when he passed but stood, belly deep, and watched him, big ears pricked forward.

Peter stopped often to rest. But he didn't mind the deep snow and hard crust. He went higher until the deer tracks finally disappeared. He decided to turn back and leaned against a stump to rest. Downslope, the trees, hanging heavy with snow, were like a Christmas card scene. He was thinking about that when he heard excited yapping from a thicket up ahead. "Dogs way up here?" he thought. Then he knew it wasn't dogs. It was coyotes, and they were chasing something. A moment later, a doe burst out of the brush. She was lunging through the snow, breaking belly deep at every jump. Her mouth was open, her tongue lolled out. She scrambled toward Peter, broke through the crust, and sprawled in the snow. She let out a terrified bawl and struggled wearily to her feet.

Two doglike animals slipped through the trees like shadows running lightly on the crust. One ear of the leading coyote hung limp as a rag. Lonesome and his mate!

Peter snapped off the safety, aimed ahead of Lonesome's nose, and pressed the trigger. Snow geysered up in front of the animal, and Lonesome skidded to a stop not thirty feet from the exhausted doe. Peter pumped in another shell and fired again. Both coyotes whirled and vanished back into the brush. "This's one doe you don't get," Peter thought. "Go catch yourselves a rabbit or some mice."

Peter stepped close to the doe. She made no effort to run but stood looking at him, unafraid, big ears jacked forward. "What's the matter with you?" he said. "Why don't you stay down in the lower country with the rest of the deer and elk and keep out of this deep snow and hard crust?".

The doe shook her head and pawed at the snow with her front feet. Peter took another step toward her. Then he saw the small knobs, the shallow, rounded depressions. "You're not a doe," he said, "you're a buck, and you've just shed your antlers." The deer shook its head and pawed the snow again. Peter began to grin. "Why, you're Bill! You sure look different without horns. You're just like a little old doe now," he said with tremendous relief.

All his fear of the buck vanished. He walked up to Bill and patted him between the ears and scratched under his chin. Bill stretched his head to receive the scratching. Peter patted his neck and sides the way Omar used to do.

"Messing around up here all alone! You're just making yourself coyote bait," he scolded. "But I guess you know that now."

Bill thrust his velvety nose against Peter's mittened hands and the boy said, "Sorry, no tobacco. If I'd known I'd find you, I'd have brought some. Come on. Let's go home and I'll get you a chew. I'll break trail for you. Remember when you led me out of the canyon to the cabin that time? Well, I'll lead you out of the snow to the cabin. Then we're even."

Peter started down the hill. Bill watched him, big ears forward. "Come on," Peter coaxed. "Let's go home." He held out his hand. Bill bobbed his head, waded to him, and nibbled hopefully at his mitten. "Just as soon as we get to the cabin, I'll give you tobacco," Peter promised. "Come on."

He went on, then stopped and looked back. Bill hadn't moved.

Once more he spoke to the deer and held out his hand. Again Bill came to him. Peter petted him and talked to him, then walked off. After the third try, Bill seemed to understand. He began following so close on the boy's heels that his nose sometimes bumped Peter's back.

Peter plowed ahead, breaking down the crust, making an easy trail for the deer. A wave of happiness came over him. He turned and patted the barren head bobbing so close. He chanted loudly a tune he made up:

"Bill, Bill, where're those horns of yours at?
You can't fight old Lonesome with nothing but that."

A couple of frightened deer lunged off through the trees. Peter laughed for no reason at all.

Bill was at his shoulder when they reached the

cabin. Peter said, "You wait here. Don't go away." He left the door open so Bill could look in while he ran into the pantry, got two squares of Star plug, and came out. He tore one into chunks and fed Bill a piece at a time. Then he coaxed Bill out to the shed. Peter fluffed up the dry grass and made a bed. Bill folded up on it with a tired sigh.

Peter sat beside him and tore up the second plug and fed it in small bites. He stayed for some time, petting Bill and talking to him.

When he finally returned to the cabin, that warm glow was still with him. Peter built up the fire and made his lunch. Afterward, he sat at the table thinking about the morning and the change there'd been in himself. It wasn't the hike, or getting out of the cabin. It had been finding Bill, and his companionship. He was no longer alone.

He remembered what Omar said, "The secret to living alone out here is to keep busy. It makes no difference if what you do is important or not. Make it important to you. And maybe if you'll look real hard, you'll discover that it is." And he'd thought Omar was a little delirious. Now he realized that Omar knew he was dying and was preparing Peter to live alone. The animals gave him something besides himself to think about. They took the place of people. They were important.

Peter knew now what he had to do. He hoped he could coax Marty and Solomon back after having neglected them so long.

141

He brought in a frozen sack of venison and cut two steaks, one for himself, the other for Marty and Solomon. He put them in the warming oven to thaw. As soon as one thawed, he cut it into inch squares and carried some out to Solomon.

The owl was perched on his usual ridge timber. He stared down at Peter with round, unwinking eyes. Peter put the meat on a post top in plain sight. He petted Bill a minute and returned to the cabin.

Peter returned to the shed just before dark. Bill had left. Solomon sat as silent and inscrutable as ever on his ridge pole. The meat on the post was untouched. Peter stirred it with a finger and coaxed, "Come and get it. I've taken the trouble to thaw it and bring it to you. The least you can do is eat it." Solomon stared at him. He didn't move.

"You're dumb!" Peter was suddenly angry. "You think you're smart, sitting up there just looking. I think you're plain dumb. Omar must have been crazy to name you Solomon." He stomped angrily out of the shed.

Peter found Marty's tracks around the base of the pine tree. He laid a trail from the base of the tree to the cabin door with the rest of the venison squares. He put the three pieces left over in the tin dish, set it just inside, and closed the door. He opened the sliding door, then stood peeking through the curtain. He saw a magpie sail out of a tree, and carry off a piece of meat. In a surprisingly short time, other birds came, and all

142

the meat disappeared. He'd have to put the meat out later, after the birds went to bed.

He sliced up the second venison steak, waited until dark, and laid the trail again. It was a bright, moonlit night, and against the white snow he saw Marty come swiftly down the tree. He dropped into the snow, sat up, and looked about. He scurried to the first chunk of meat and ate it. Then the next and next. He was within a few feet of the cabin door when he stopped and sat up suspiciously. The next moment he disappeared around the corner of the cabin.

Peter thought of the lighted window. Marty always came after they'd gone to bed and the cabin was dark. Maybe the light frightened him. Peter built up the fire again, banked it, turned out the light, and went to bed. He lay waiting to hear the rattle of the tin pan. He went to sleep waiting.

When Peter awoke in the morning, the fire was out, the room was cold as outdoors, and the pieces of venison were still in the pan. Marty had not returned.

Peter made extra biscuits for breakfast and afterward carried them out to the shed to check on Bill. The deer was lying in the grass bed. He fed Bill and sat beside him. He petted Bill and talked to him several minutes.

Solomon was perched on his timber, staring inscrutably down at him. The two pieces of meat were gone from the post. He returned to the cabin, got the meat Marty hadn't eaten, and put it on the post for the owl.

143

He cut another steak, thawed it, and waited for night.

Bill came from the shed in the afternoon. Peter called him and fed him some small pieces of tobacco. When Bill nudged his hand for more, Peter said, "Nothing doing. You had two whole plugs yesterday. We've got to make this last till spring."

Bill went plowing off through the snow. But Peter was sure he'd return.

He thought about Solomon while he waited for dark. The owl was used to having Omar call him from the shed. When it was dusk, Peter got out the heavy leather glove, took several pieces of venison, and stood in the same spot Omar had. He tried to imitate the low, soft call that Omar used. But he could not remember the exact tone. He did his best and sent the soft sound into the night. He waited a minute, then whistled again, and again. No Solomon. Peter kept trying until the cold got into him.

He returned to the cabin. His call hadn't fooled Solomon, or maybe the owl had already forgotten the tryst he'd kept with Omar nightly.

Peter filled the stove, and began preparing for Marty's visit. He had the meat sliced and in the tin when he heard the lonesome *whoo-whoo-ooo* from the pine tree. He grabbed the glove, several pieces of venison, eased the door open, and stepped out. Against the clear night sky he saw the black blob that was Solomon sitting on the limb. He slowly approached the tree. He was almost to the spot where Omar usually stood when Solomon sailed off the limb and disappeared among the trees. He waited, but the owl did not return.

Peter went to the cabin disappointed. He was waiting for Marty's visit when he realized his mistake. Solomon always sat on the limb, and he and Omar talked back and forth several times before he'd fly down and take the meat. Maybe the owl had been waiting for him to talk. When he hadn't, Solomon knew it wasn't Omar and flew away. If he could coax him back tomorrow night, he'd not make that mistake.

Peter scattered the meat from the foot of the pine to the cabin door again. He went inside, closed the door, put the tin dish on the floor, turned out the light, and went to bed. He lay there listening intently for a long time. He'd about given up hope and was dropping off to sleep when the rattling of the dish brought him wide awake. He turned his head carefully and made out Marty's sleek shape. Peter smiled in the darkness.

The next night, he prepared for Solomon again. He stood in the exact spot and called. His call was not good, but he hoped he was improving. On his fourth try Solomon ghosted from the shed and lit on the limb.

Peter waited, holding the morsel of venison on his outstretched gloved hand. Solomon called. It was a soft, hollow sound, each note distinctly separate at the beginning, then running together at the end. They formed one long *oooo,* coming faster and faster until they faded into nothing.

Peter pursed his lips and reached for the same ef-

145

fect. He didn't quite find it and held his breath for fear Solomon would fly away. Solomon remained and finally answered. Peter tried again. By bringing the air up from the depths of his chest he kept the tone soft and gave it that hollow everywhere-nowhere carrying sound.

Solomon answered but did not move. They talked back and forth twice more. Peter's arm was getting tired, and he was cold. Then, so quickly he was hardly aware it had happened, the shadow sailed from the limb, swept over him with ghostly silence, banked, and came down over his outstretched hand. For an instant, the owl seemed to hesitate in the air, then he was back on the limb. Peter had felt nothing, but the piece of venison was gone. He held out a second piece. They talked several times. Then Solomon repeated the performance.

Peter went into the cabin smiling. They were all back, Bill, Marty, and Solomon. He'd make out fine. He was no longer alone. Nothing could hurt him now.

12

"If you thought Omar was a little crazy the way he talked to these animals, you should hear yourself," Peter thought. "You're a blabbermouth. To anybody else you'd sound completely mad."

Peter looked ahead to his evening conversations with Solomon. He felt his owl call was now as good as Omar's. About the second call each night, Solomon would fly silently from the shed and light on the limb of the pine tree. He and Peter would then hold lengthy conversations. In his mind Peter had put words to them. His first calls to Solomon meant something like, "Come a-running, or a-flying. It's time to eat."

Solomon's soft answer from the tree limb would mean, "So okay, here I am. Let's get at it."

"You're always hungry. Here it is."

"Venison again! Omar used to catch me nice fat mice."

"Not in winter. You've got to wait until spring."

"But I get tired of the same old thing all the time. Why don't you change once in a while?"

"You wouldn't eat anything else, and you know it."

"You've never tried me."

"I'm not going to."

"Oh, all right. Hold it out. Here I come!"

After Solomon had eaten, Peter would look at the dark lump on the limb and call softly, "Omar used to say you were very smart. I'm not so sure."

"Got you hand-feeding me, haven't I?"

"That's no proof. And just sitting up there looking wise doesn't prove a thing."

"No? Well, I stay in the shed where it's warm, and you stand out here in the cold and wait for me. And I come when I'm good and ready. You can't call that stupid."

"All right. So maybe you are as wise as you look," Peter would agree.

"That's the smartest thing you've said tonight," Solomon would say. Then he'd sail off the limb and disappear.

Peter would return to the cabin feeling good. He could discuss things with Solomon. With Bill and Marty the conversations were always one-sided.

Sometimes Bill was a pest. Before taking off into the timber to browse for the day, he'd stand in front of the cabin, shaking his hornless head and stamping his feet until Peter came out. When Bill returned at night, they went through the same ritual before he'd go into the shed.

Bill often accompanied Peter on hikes. Peter would take the rifle, a pocketful of jerky, some tobacco cut

148

into small pieces, and they'd be off. Bill walked beside him nudging his pocket, and Peter would dole out the tobacco sparingly so it lasted until they got back. Sometimes Bill wandered off to nibble at succulent buds or to investigate. Then he'd hurry to catch up.

Peter wanted one of the animals in the cabin for company during the long evenings. He'd read about a tame deer that lived in the house with a family, so with tobacco he coaxed Bill inside. The deer was not startled. It was a little like the shed. He wandered about, his curious black nose lifted, snorting delicately as he sampled all the strange smells. But Peter hadn't realized he was quite so big. He could reach the top shelves. He thrust his nose against the coffee can and knocked it off, spilling coffee across the floor. Peter grabbed the can and scooped up the coffee. He wiped cans of beans and pears off the shelf. Peter had barely retrieved these when Bill was nudging the lamp on the table. He grabbed for the lamp as it teetered dangerously. Then he shooed Bill outside.

Peter could not tame Marty. After much careful work, he did manage to get Marty inside while the light was lit. With fresh tidbits of meat he coaxed him to within a few feet. But Peter didn't dare try to touch him. Marty would edge toward a bit of meat an inch at a time, then sit up and study Peter with beady eyes. Peter could hold him for a few brief moments while he talked to him in his quietest voice, "I won't try to make a house cat of you. But I am glad to see you. What do you do, sleep all day? Then run around all night? I wish you'd come in sometime during the day. You always act half starved, but I know you're not. All right, you've got your stomach full. I'll see you tomorrow night."

The cold weather held steady for days. Then, a degree at a time, it began to moderate. The snow line crept back up the slope. The deer and elk followed. Peter had checked off February on the calendar, then March. Bill's new horns began to grow, covered with soft velvet. He shook his head menacingly at Peter, but now the boy only laughed and patted his sides. The remainder of the venison hanging in the pine tree began to thaw. He finally took it down, hid it in a snowbank, and piled rocks over it.

April came in blustery. Several times Peter was sure they were in for another blizzard. Storms swept down off the high ridges and closed his world to swirling snow. But in a day or so, it was gone again. There were good days when he was sure spring was coming. Then it froze and laid a blanket of ice over everything. He used the last of the frozen venison. Mice became active above ground. He set the traps again. Bill's tobacco was getting low. The jerky was holding up best of all. He had two full cans left.

Spring came to the canyon as it never had in the city. Peter saw the first wedge of geese go over, their calls drifting down through the silence. One day a flight of ducks fled upriver searching for a spot of quiet water. A green tinge began to show through the dead brown of winter's ground cover and along the barren branches of maple, hazel, and aspen. As the leaves grew, Peter's view of the river from the cabin was gradually cut off. Bill left for higher ground where the browse was better. Sometimes he'd be gone for several days. One day Peter realized the snow line was almost as far up the slope as it had been when he came last fall. The crust had become soft and porous. Countless threadlike streams trickled out from the base and wriggled downhill. The earth was like a water-filled sponge. Then Peter saw how that fine network of tiny roots from shrubs and low ground cover held the soil from slipping downward into the boiling river.

The sun was working higher in the sky. Daylight hours were lengthening noticeably. Bill's horns were half grown and gave promise of a fine rack of antlers. But Bill was being very careful and usually stayed out of the thick brush because his antlers were soft and could be easily broken.

One day Peter noticed that some of the big rocks in the river were almost covered. The normally crystal blue water had turned dirty gray. A few days later, it was coffee brown, and the rocks had disappeared. Soon the river would be deep enough for the jet boats. The steady rise of the river brought his home and parents closer each day. Excitement began to build within him until he could hardly stand it. He'd go hiking to work it off.

One morning Peter went up to Omar's grave. Surprisingly few weeds had grown up between the rocks. It took but a few minutes to clean it. He spent more

151

time on Edward Dennis's grave and replaced some rocks. He had just finished when he became conscious of a foreign sound. He realized he'd been hearing it for several minutes. He looked up, searching the blue sky. There it was, high up the slope, a little above the snow line, skimming the tops of the trees like an eagle.

A plane!

Peter leaped to his feet and dashed for the cabin. He kept thinking, "I haven't got a fire pile. How can I attract their attention?" He raced into the cabin, saw the white sack he'd kept the fresh venison in, grabbed it, and tore outside.

The plane was flying back and forth, working downhill. It was almost over the cabin. He waved the sack frantically and shouted at the top of his lungs. The plane passed over, made a leisurely turn, and came back. Peter continued waving and shouting. The plane passed directly over him and he read the big printed letters on the side, MOUNTAIN HOME LOGGING COMPANY. There were two men in the plane. They both waved. The plane turned, flew straight up the slope, over the high ridge, and disappeared.

Peter looked at the spot where it had vanished. He kept telling himself, "In a minute it'll come back. It'll fly right down this slope to me and drop a note telling me they know who I am and that a rescue team is on the way." But the plane didn't return. Disappointment settled in the pit of his stomach and threatened to make him sick.

Finally his depression began to wear off. It wasn't

as if he wouldn't be rescued, he told himself. It was simply that this was the first sign of any possible chance to get out in months. It wasn't the fault of the people in the plane. He had no fire pile. To them he was someone waving "Hello" to the first humans he'd seen since last fall. They'd been low enough to know he wasn't Omar, if they'd known the old man. Maybe they thought that Omar had company. He felt better after reasoning it out.

He began building another fire pile in front of the cabin. Then, suddenly, he had an idea he'd never thought of all these months. He gathered the biggest rocks he could manage and spelled out HELP in a cleared spot. By nightfall he was ready if another plane came.

The warm weather held. The snow line continued to retreat. Peter knew the thawing he saw around him extended to more than two hundred miles of river above, draining thousands of square miles of watershed. The river crawled halfway up the bank toward the cabin. It had been fast before; it was a millrace now. Peter didn't see how any boat could fight its way through this mud-brown, charging water. He watched the river anxiously. The first jet might come any time.

He was eating lunch, with the door open to the early spring sunshine, when the roaring came from the river. At first he credited the sound to the river itself. Then he knew better. He dashed out down the trail to where he could see the broad expanse. The jet, a red-and-white cork on the water, was far out and had already passed. It was heading upriver toward the great shoulder of rock ahead. Peter raced to the water's edge, yelling at the top of his lungs.

There were three people in the boat, but they were all looking straight ahead. He knew his voice didn't carry above the jet noise and the roar of the river. The boat slammed into the water like a bucking horse, throwing spray so high and thick that at times he couldn't see it. The boat disappeared around the shoulder of rock.

Peter watched the river a few minutes, then turned back to the cabin. Omar had said the jets stopped here. This one hadn't. He had to do something to be sure he attracted attention. He'd make a big sign that he could set up on the riverbank.

He took two white flour sacks, ripped them open, and sewed the ends together to make a banner almost six feet long by two feet wide. He could find no paint, so he took a bottle of ketchup and painted HELP the full height and length of the banner. He fastened the ends to two long sticks that he could drive into the ground. Carrying this and the ax, he headed down the trail to the river.

The moment he came in sight of the water, he stopped. He just stood there. Two jet boats were pulled up on the bank and a half-dozen men stood about. Two were coming up the path toward him.

13

Peter just stood there holding the stakes and his rolled-up sign. One of the men was young and slender, with black, curly hair. The other was much older, close to Omar's age, he guessed. He was stocky and broad-chested. He carried an old hat in one hand. His head was bald except for a thin rim of white hair around his ears. He had a small, neat, gray moustache, a blunt, stubborn chin, and the bluest eyes.

The young man said, "Well, I didn't know Omar had company all winter. I'm Harry Thomas. I own these two jets. This is Senator Mike Kaufman."

Peter had heard of Senator Kaufman, and he'd seen his picture many times. Bulldog Kaufman, they called him, because he never quit in a fight. "He's a tough, honest old man who's owned by no one," Peter's father once said. "I don't always agree with him, but I admire him."

These thoughts raced through Peter's mind, but at the moment, they refused to register. All he could think was that at long last the waiting was over. He'd be going home. For a moment his throat was too thick to talk. His eyes blurred. His first words were not what he meant to say. "That other boat didn't stop. They didn't even look this way. I yelled and yelled but they went right on up the river and disappeared. I was making a sign. I didn't hear you come."

"We were running half-throttle here close to shore," Thomas explained. "Omar never told me he had relatives."

Peter shook his head. "I'm Pete Grayson. We—we crashed in the canyon last fall."

"Crashed! You and Omar? You mean in a plane? What was Omar doing in a plane?" Thomas glanced about. "Where is Omar?"

"He's dead," Peter said. "So's Frank Eldridge. I've been waiting and waiting."

The senator said gently, "Why don't we go up to the cabin and you can tell us all about it?"

They sat at the table, and Peter told them everything from the day the plane crashed.

"Grayson Electronics," the senator said. "I remember. George Grayson had the air full of planes for weeks. His son was lost on a flight last fall. So you're George Grayson's son. Your folks are going to be two mighty happy people, young man."

"Yes, sir," Peter said.

"I can't believe it," Thomas shook his head, "Omar dead. Why, he was as much a part of this canyon as the rock. I thought he'd go on forever." He looked at Peter, "Did he fall or something?"

"He saved a doe from drowning. She broke through the ice. I guess he got pneumonia. He died after the first of the year. I buried him alongside the other grave that's a couple of hundred feet from here."

"Saving a deer. That sounds like Omar." Thomas rose. "I know where that other grave is. Think I'll have a look."

Senator Kaufman's blue eyes studied Peter, "You've had a mighty rough winter for a boy. But you've come through fine."

"Omar taught me a lot," Peter said, "but I couldn't have made it without Bill and Solomon and Marty."

"Then you weren't alone."

"Bill's a mule deer, Solomon's an owl, and Marty is a marten. They're my friends."

"I'd like to meet them," the senator said, smiling. "But right now I want to take a hike up through this timber. I imagine you know the area pretty well, eh?" And when Peter nodded, "How'd you like to come along as guide?"

"Fine." Peter got the rifle, stuffed a couple pieces of jerky into his pocket automatically, then doubtfully held the can out to the senator. "It doesn't look so good," he started to explain.

"Jerky!" the senator took two pieces. He cut off a generous chunk and stuffed it into his mouth. "Haven't had any since I was a kid."

"You know about jerky?" Peter asked.

"Know about it! I was practically raised on it. My folks lived in a little jerkwater town in the southern

157

part of the state. Post office and store. We were the whole town. We had jerky all the time."

There were four squares of Star plug tobacco left, and Peter put one in his pocket.

Senator Kaufman smiled, and Peter explained, "It's for Bill, if we happen to see him."

"When I was fifteen, my best friend chewed," the senator said. "I tried chewing and got sick. Well, let's go."

The rest of the party were unloading sleeping bags and gear at the boats. The senator called, "Pete and I are going for a walk. See you later."

A couple shouted back, "Want any company?"

"Nope." And to Peter as they walked off through the trees, "No sense taking them. They're just along for the ride." The senator kept looking about, muttering, "What a stand of timber! No wonder they want to log it."

"Do you mean the Mountain Home Logging Company?" Peter asked.

"You know about them?"

"Their plane was over a few days ago. Omar said they came up in two big jet boats last summer and looked over the timber. You're not going to let them log it, are you?"

"That's why I'm up here," the senator explained. "There's the logging company that wants to cut the timber. But a number of organizations and clubs want it declared a wilderness area and left as it is. There'll be a hearing on it in Washington. I want to see this timber and collect some facts. I'm chairman of that committee."

"When is the hearing?"

"Two weeks from today."

"What will they do at the hearing?"

"There'll be people from both sides. Those representing the logging company, who want to log the land, and others representing clubs, organizations, and such. They don't want it logged. Each side will present its case. The committee will listen, then render the decision that it thinks is best for the country." He squinted blue eyes at Peter. "Something tells me you don't want this land logged."

"I don't!" Peter said. "And neither did Omar. He lived here for fifty years. He knew a lot about the country, and he said it would be terrible."

"In what way, Pete?"

Peter shook his head, suddenly embarrassed at his boldness before a United States senator. "Just things," he mumbled, "Omar could have told you. He talked about it a lot. He was going to use his gold dust to hire a lawyer and try to stop them."

"Omar's not here, and you are." The senator studied him a moment. "Pete," he said quietly, "I told you I grew up in a jerkwater town. It wasn't really a town. There were about thirty people. My first school was an old building that held twelve desks and a potbellied stove. We boys had to pack wood for it. You don't need to be embarrassed with me. I just represent the people, and you're one of them. I can't do my job un-

159

less I get all of the information possible on a subject."

"I wish Omar was here."

"So do I. I need to know the kinds of things he could tell me. It's his testimony this committee in Washington should hear. But we have to do what's next best. You tell me what he said."

Peter still hesitated.

"It's your duty as a citizen to pass Omar's knowledge on to me, Pete, so I can make the right decision when the time comes."

"Well," Peter said, "Omar said it took hundreds of years, maybe as many as a thousand, for this forest to grow like it is. If it's logged off the way Mountain Home Logging Company does it, this will be a wasteland. There will never be a forest here again."

"Never's a long time, Pete. Trees grow pretty fast."

"Not on this land. It's very poor soil. Hill land is never good. It washes easily during heavy rains and spring thaws. Omar said it takes as long as two to three hundred years for nature to build up one inch of good topsoil. And you need topsoil to grow things."

"Then if this is logged off. . . ?"

"Omar said big machines, ways of logging and building logging roads will tear up all these fine roots that are holding the soil now. When the rains and thaws come, the water runoff will wash this topsoil into the river. This land will be cut by deep gullies and ditches. All the wild game and birds will disappear because there will be nothing for them to eat and no places to hide or nest and raise their young."

160

The senator nodded, "What else did Omar say?"

"Omar said dozens of streams originate in this forest and drain into the river. Some are big salmon-spawning streams. If this land is scalped. . . ."

"You mean clear-cut?"

Peter nodded. "These spawning streams will dry up, or the silt washing into them will cover the spawning beds. The salmon will no longer have any place to lay their eggs. The salmon run could stop forever in the river."

"Omar was sure of all this, Pete?"

"He said there used to be another forest similar to this one about forty miles downriver. It was called the Flat Iron Creek area. It was logged off years ago by the same Mountain Home Logging Company. There were several big spawning streams there, but they've dried up now. They're just rock beds. The topsoil has drained off, and the land has been cut by washes and gullies. Omar said it looks like a war had been fought there. There's no game. Only a few chukars and grouse."

"Speaking of game," the senator said, "I don't see any."

"The deer and elk are further up toward the snow line where the browse is better. We're only a couple hundred yards from the river now. It's almost a mile. If you feel up to it. . . ."

The senator took off his hat and patted his bald dome. "The shingles are mostly gone, Pete. But the boiler's still full of steam. Let's go."

The senator cut off a chunk of jerky and crammed it into his mouth. Then they started up the slope. Peter began softly whistling "The Big Rock Candy Mountains."

"Hey!" the senator said, "you'll scare the game, Pete. I want to see it."

"I'm just letting them know we're coming."

"So they'll hightail it out of the country ahead of us," the senator complained.

"No they won't."

"When I hunted as a young sprout, we went as quietly as possible or we didn't get a shot."

"You're going to see game," Peter promised. "We're not hunting." He continued whistling.

"That's a mighty old tune," the senator said finally. "What's it called?"

Peter told him.

"Sure, I remember now. Never did know the words though. You know 'em, Pete?"

"I know the ones Omar taught me."

"Sing 'em."

"I'm not very good."

"There's just you and me and these animals we're supposed to see. Let 'er rip, Pete."

Peter began to sing:

"In The Big Rock Candy Mountains,
There's a land that's fair and bright,"

When he finished the first verse, the senator was

humming along with him. "That's good, Pete. You know any more?"

"I know a couple."

"Tell me the words, and let me get my teeth into that thing with you."

Peter gave him the words as they walked along beneath the trees up the gently rising slope.

"Got it," the senator nodded. "Okay, let's hit it." The senator kept time, waving his hand like a baton while he sang in what had once been a barbershop baritone. Halfway through, his enthusiasm ran away with him. He threw back his head and bellowed the last lines at the top of his lungs. When they finished, he looked guiltily at Peter.

"We just want to let the game know we're around," Peter explained, "not scare them clear out of the country."

"Sorry. I used to sing in a quartet when I was young," the senator explained sheepishly. "Haven't let go on a good ballad song in more'n thirty years. Why, that took me back to—to when I had hair, Pete. I'll muffle the next one a little. You said you knew another verse."

Peter gave him the words as they walked, then they sang together. Peter tried to blend his young voice with the senator's.

He'd almost made it when they ended:

"Oh, come with me, and we'll go see
The Big Rock Candy Mountains."

163

"Whew!" the senator stopped, took off his hat, and wiped his face. "That runs into work, walking and singing, too. How come a young feller like you sings an oldie like that, instead of this modern bang-bang stuff?"

"That's what Omar taught me, and it was all he knew," Peter said. "And the way the words rhyme, and the tune, somehow they seem right for out here."

"I'm inclined to agree. You know any more?"

"Omar taught me a couple verses of 'Down in the Valley.' He sang that a lot."

"No kidding," the senator laughed.

They came to the edge of a small grassy meadow and Peter pointed. Five cow elk and a bull stood in the center, all heads turned, looking straight at them. "They heard us," Peter explained. "They knew what to expect. If we'd sneaked up on them, it would have startled them, and they'd have been gone in a flash."

"Son of a gun," the senator exclaimed. "How about that!"

A little further on, Peter pointed out three does and a young buck. Beyond them, a couple of young bucks. Then more deer and elk. There were chipmunks, squirrels, and a variety of birds.

"A regular Garden of Eden, so help me," the senator murmured. "I had no idea there was so much game in here. And the size of these trees! You don't find many places like this any more."

"That's because there are no roads and it's so hard to get into. There aren't even many hunters in the fall.

164

The jet boats can't run then to bring them in. Omar used to say this was his forest and his animals," Peter said. "After fifty years he said he claimed squatter's rights."

"I don't blame him."

They went on again, but Senator Kaufman was saving his breath for climbing. Peter began to whistle. In the next half mile they saw more game. But by the time they reached the snow line, the animals were gone.

Peter showed the senator the small rivulets of water snaking downhill. He pointed out how the root system of trees, brush, and low ground cover held the thin topsoil.

"I see," the senator nodded. "I see."

They rested side by side on a log. The senator said, "Thomas tells me this forest runs upriver for miles."

"That's what Omar said."

A cool breeze funneled down off the high peaks. The sun fell behind the distant gorge rim. "Not much use going any higher and getting into this snow," the senator said. "I've seen enough."

"When will the boats be going back downriver?" Peter asked.

"We'll leave early and take a short run upriver for a look, then head back down. You'll be talking with your parents tomorrow night, Pete." He rose. "Maybe we'd better start back."

They entered a small clearing and a huge buck deer started toward them. He shook his head and pawed the ground.

The senator stopped, "Pete, that fellow means business. Shoot ahead of him and scare him off. Hurry!"

"That's Bill!" Peter said, pleased. "Here, Bill. Come on. Come and get it." Peter twisted a small piece of tobacco from the plug and held it out.

Bill walked up to him, lifted it, and stood eating while Peter rubbed his ears and patted his neck. "Haven't seen you for a couple of days. I was about to come looking for you."

"He's quite an animal!" the senator said. "About the biggest mulie I've ever seen."

Bill nudged Peter's hand, looking for more tobacco. Peter twisted off another piece and said, "Would you like to feed him, sir?"

"Sure would." The senator held the piece in his palm. Bill lifted it delicately and stood chewing while the senator patted his neck and scratched his batlike ears. Peter gave the senator the rest of the plug. He tore it up and fed Bill. "You like that, huh? Not afraid tobacco'll stunt your growth? When I was a kid, we said it would."

They started downgrade and Bill followed, nudging the senator for more. When none was forthcoming, he finally turned off and disappeared among the trees. The senator looked after Bill and asked, "You got any more wild pets like him, Pete?"

"Solomon and Marty."

"I remember. The owl and the marten. Do I get to see 'em?"

166

"Yes, sir. We'll feed them tonight."

"Good! Good!" The senator was still in a ballad-singing mood. "Maybe we should end this sing-along with another tune," he suggested. "How about 'Down in the Valley'?"

"Okay," Peter said.

They began to sing softly:

"Down in the valley, valley so low,
Hang your head over, hear the wind blow.
Hear the wind blow, dear.
Hear the wind blow.
Hang your head over,
Hear the wind blow.

Writing this letter containing three lines,
Answer my question: Will you be mine?
Will you be mine, dear. Will you be mine?
Answer my question? Will you be mine?

Build me a castle forty feet high,
So I can see her as she goes by;
As she goes by, dear, as she goes by,
So I can see her as she goes by."

They came out finally near the cabin. The rest of the party was inside. Harry Thomas was cooking dinner. He had steaks on the stove and a dozen fresh ones waiting on the table. He grinned at Peter. "I took the liberty of using your stove instead of a campfire."

"That's fine," Peter said. "Could I have a small piece of that fresh meat for Solomon and Marty?"

"Take a whole steak. We brought plenty."

After dinner, all but the senator repaired to the boats to spend the night. The senator's sleeping bag had been put on Omar's bed.

Darkness came quickly. Peter lit the lamp and cut the steak into squares. He got the leather glove and asked the senator, "Would you like to feed Solomon?"

"You mean by hand, like Bill?"

"Of course. You won't feel a thing."

"Well, okay. You seem to have all your fingers. What do I do?"

Peter explained how he called the owl, where the senator should stand, and how to hold the meat.

"All set," the senator said. "Gimme the call."

Peter stood in the shadow of the cabin and whistled softly. "Sounds like an owl, all right," the senator said. "Don't know if I can even whistle any more or not."

The senator's call was not a good mimic. Peter said, "You hold out the meat. I'll call him from here."

On the second call, Solomon ghosted silently from the shed and lit in the pine tree. Peter called again. Solomon answered. Peter waited, then called. One moment the owl was a motionless black blob, the next he swooped low over the senator. He seemed to hesitate in the air at the fingers of the outstretched glove. Then he flapped silently back to the limb.

The senator said in a low voice, "Son of a gun! I never felt a thing."

"Hold out the next one," Peter said softly.

Peter called twice more, and Solomon answered each time. Then he sailed down and took the second piece of meat.

"That's all," Peter said. "He'll go off hunting now."

They returned to the cabin, and the senator asked, "What about that other animal you told me about, the marten?"

"He'll be coming soon," Peter said. He put fresh steak in the tin dish, set it in the usual place, and closed the door. He dimmed the lamp a little. Then he and the senator sat side by side at the table. "We'll have to be very quiet," Peter explained. "It's about time. Whatever you do, don't move. He's used to seeing just me."

"You think he'll come in with this light burning and us sitting here?" the senator asked. "But I thought martens were very shy."

"They are. But Marty'll come," Peter said confidently.

"If I hadn't already fed an owl and a deer, I wouldn't believe you," the senator muttered.

They sat there a long time, then the senator finally whispered. "Maybe all these people being around scared him off."

Peter had to agree that maybe they had. He was disappointed and about to call it off when the senator nudged him. Marty had entered and picked up a piece of meat. Peter waited until he was almost finished, then said softly, "You're late tonight."

Marty sat up, beady eyes fastened on Peter. His black nose twitched. "This is the last handout you're going to get." Peter bent forward carefully and tossed a small piece of steak under his nose. Marty immediately swallowed it. Peter tossed another and another, each bringing the marten closer. With the last piece, Marty was only a yard or so away. "That's all," Peter said. "From now on, you'll have to do all your own hunting. You can go now, Marty. Goodbye."

Marty sat and studied Peter a few seconds. Then in a twinkling, he whirled, raced across the floor, and vanished out the trap door.

Peter looked at the hole, and his own words came home to him with a shock. He had talked to Marty and fed him for the last time. Bill and Solomon, too. Tomorrow he'd be going home, leaving here forever.

Senator Kaufman said quietly, "Now I've seen everything. This has been an afternoon and evening like I never expected to see again. It took me back a lot of years. Thanks, Pete, for more than you'll ever know. I think I'll turn in. This night I should sleep like a baby."

But Peter could not sleep. He lay listening to the soft sounds of the night and was surprised at how well he understood them. He thought he heard Solomon once. But it could have been another owl. He could hear the endless rumble of the river. That single branch scratched across the roof as it always did when a breeze disturbed it. Faintly he heard Lonesome and his mate far above the snow line. He smiled, remembering he'd once believed it a wolf call. He thought of home and his mother and father, and a terrible urgency to be gone came over him. With it was mingled a sadness at leaving. He was all mixed up.

They ate breakfast in the cabin, and afterward the senator announced they'd run upriver, look at the timber, and return before noon. "Then we'll head home, Pete," he said. "Do you want to go up with us, or do you have things to get ready here before you leave?"

"I've got things to do," Peter said. "I'll wait for you to come back."

As soon as they were gone, Peter got out his sleeping bag, packed in Omar's poke of gold dust and Frank Eldridge's billfold and papers. He got his suitcase and Omar's old rifle and carried them down to the riverbank. Omar's clothing would have to stay. He went up to Omar's grave, carefully weeded it, and replaced several rocks.

Peter used the remainder of the time baking a huge batch of biscuits. That used up all the sourdough. He took some out to the shed and left them for Bill along with the three plugs of tobacco that were left. There was just enough jerky left to fill his pockets.

He stood in the middle of the kitchen and looked about. He'd taken care of everything he could. Then he remembered one last thing. He took out the calendar, marked off the day, and returned it to the drawer. He went out and closed the door.

When the jet boats returned, he was sitting on the riverbank, waiting.

They loaded his stuff aboard, backed into the swift channel, and were off with a roar. Peter stood in the stern, gripping the rail. The last moment, he thought he caught a glimpse of Bill walking out of the trees. But he wasn't sure.

🌲🌲🌲🌲🌲🌲🌲　14　🌲🌲🌲🌲🌲🌲🌲

The two jet boats roared out of the canyon while the sun was still up. Senator Kaufman and Peter hunted up a telephone, and he called his parents. Then the senator rushed him to a small airport where he caught a plane for home.

The last thing Peter said to the senator was, "Do you think you can save Omar's wilderness, sir?"

" 'Omar's Wilderness'—that's a good name for it, Pete. I don't know. As I said before, it all depends on the facts presented by the people who appear before the committee. Rest assured we'll do our best."

His parents met him at the airport. His mother clung to him and cried, "I knew you were alive! I always knew it!" His father was too choked up to talk, but the hug he gave Peter almost cracked his ribs.

A flashbulb went off in Peter's face. Then another and another. The press was here. Peter looked at his father, who shrugged. "We didn't call them. Maybe somebody on one of the jet boats did."

A pair of reporters were there with notebooks. The questions began to fly:

"What happened to the plane?"

"How long were you lost? Six months! Wow!"

"Did you live alone all that time?"

"Who's Omar Pickett?"

"You had to bury him! Alone!"

"How'd you keep from going crazy all those months?"

"Bill, Marty, and Solomon. Then you weren't alone."

"They're animals? You're kidding."

There were more pictures—of his father and mother—his parents greeting him. It was fifteen minutes before they got away and ran for the car.

The first few minutes at home were bedlam. They were all talking and laughing, crying a little, and firing questions no one bothered to answer. Finally it quieted down somewhat, and his mother took command as she always did in the house. She herded Peter and his father into the big beamed living room, then she scurried about bringing in trays of sandwiches, coffee, and milk.

Peter looked through the big windows at the million lights of the city below, the pattern of the streets, and the headlights of the moving traffic. Everything was just as he remembered it.

"We were so excited when your call came, neither of us could eat," his mother explained.

"I haven't eaten either," Peter said.

174

They sat and ate and talked. Clara Grayson's sharp eyes kept poring over her son. "You're so brown. Your hands never had callouses before."

"I've been working, Mom. Split my own wood, did all the cooking, everything. I can whip up a pretty good meal, including sourdough bread, biscuits, or cake."

"That's why you're heavier," she said, smiling. "You're taller, too."

"He's got muscles under that shirt." George Grayson laughed. "I felt 'em."

"You've changed a lot." His mother's eyes were probing. "You're not a fifteen-year-old boy any more, Peter. You—you're a young man." She said it almost sadly.

"You can't spend a winter in that canyon and not change," Peter said. "You're both looking swell."

"Feeling swell—now," his father said.

Finally lunch was over, the trays were returned to the kitchen. The small talk was ended.

"Now," George Grayson said, "let's have the whole story from the time you got into the plane with Frank to fly to the ranch till your phone call this afternoon."

Peter began to talk. He took them quickly through the wreck, how he followed Bill to Omar's cabin, the burial of Frank Eldridge.

"You mean that terrible old man made you help bury Frank?" his mother demanded. "That was horrible."

"It was good sense, Mom."

175

He told of the days waiting for a plane, his attempt to escape downriver, and how Omar had rescued him.

"That took raw courage," his father murmured. "I'd like to have met Omar."

Peter covered their living together, how he learned to cook, and Omar's companions—Bill, Marty, and Solomon.

His mother said, "It sounds like the Garden of Eden or something."

He described their first blizzard, the trick of rolling your socks to keep the snow out of your shoes. "You've got to keep your feet dry in that below-zero weather. That's the main thing." He told them of Omar's death and could not, even now, keep the thickness from his throat.

"You lived all alone out there in that wilderness after that," his mother said. "No wonder you've changed."

"Not alone, Mom. I had Marty, Bill, and Solomon. All the things Omar taught me not only kept me alive but saved me from getting cabin fever."

Peter filled them in right down to the arrival of the jet boats. "This is all I brought out." He indicated the rifle, sleeping bag, gold-dust poke, and billfold. "Everything else I left in the cabin just as it was—clothing, blankets on the bed, food in the pantry."

There were tears in Clara Grayson's eyes. "Omar must have been a wonderful person. I love him, just from hearing you talk about him."

George Grayson ran fingers nervously through his

straight black hair. "All that in six months!" He shook his head. "And I thought I'd had some pretty big adventures. You've already lived a big chunk of life, Peter."

"I guess so. Dad, Omar and Senator Kaufman called me Pete."

His father nodded, "That figures. You like it?"

"Yes."

"So do I."

"Well, I don't," Clara Grayson said emphatically.

"I'll see that Frank's wife gets the billfold tomorrow," George Grayson said. "Now what shall we do with Omar's gold dust? Didn't you say he had no family?"

Peter nodded. "He meant to fight Mountain Home Logging Company with it. But Senator Kaufman says it's not necessary. A number of organizations are already fighting to have that whole region turned into a wilderness area."

"We can have the dust assayed and put in the bank under a special account. If the hearing goes well, then you can decide what to do with it."

Clara Grayson said, "Even if the hearing goes badly and Mountain Home logs the timber, they won't tear down the cabin, and they don't dare touch those graves. Why not set the money aside as a fund to care for them?"

"Omar would like that."

"Then we'll do it," George Grayson said.

The important questions were out of the way. They

177

talked a long time. The family warmth and companionship that Peter had missed so much folded around him. There were six months of family catching-up to cover.

"We didn't celebrate Christmas," his mother said. "We didn't have the heart. We did have Frank Eldridge's wife and little girl over for dinner."

"Didn't celebrate New Year's either," George Grayson added. "Didn't even step out on the porch to listen to the whistles. Been mighty quiet around here."

"Christmas went by, and I didn't know it," Peter said. "But we sure celebrated New Year's." He told them how Omar fired the rifle and described the party they had. "Omar said it was the first New Year's party he'd been to in fifty years."

Finally, Clara Grayson began to yawn. "Do you two realize what time it is? Tomorrow's almost here. I'm going to bed." She kissed Peter and hugged him again. "Tonight I'm going to sleep, really sleep."

Peter carried the sleeping bag, his father held the rifle, and they climbed the stairs. His room was big and airy. His high school pennant was on the wall. His books were a neat row on the desk.

"Your mother wouldn't let anyone touch a thing. She knew you'd be back. She's an amazing woman, Pete."

Peter put the sleeping bag in the closet. His father kept turning the old rifle in his hands. "Mighty well cared for. A 30-30 long barrel. Must be at least fifty

178

years old. Would you like to put it in the trophy room?"

"I think Omar would rather I kept it here in the bedroom."

George Grayson laid the rifle on a chair. "Little light for big game."

"My new rifle was smashed in the plane wreck."

"I'll get you another."

"I don't want one. I'm not much of a hunter, Dad."

"Turned against it, eh?"

"I was never for it. I couldn't tell you before. But I don't want to go up to the ranch and hunt game that's fenced in. It's not my idea of sport."

"You have changed. Well, I've changed a little, too. After you disappeared, I couldn't go back to the ranch. Didn't even want to think about it. I sort of figured it was partly to blame for your disappearance. I pulled out of it. The others are selling it to a fellow who's going to turn it into a cattle ranch."

"Good."

George Grayson hesitated in the doorway. "Having you home safe and sound is the finest thing that ever happened to me." He smiled. "I've an idea that getting to know this new Pete Grayson is going to be a lot of fun. Good night."

Peter stretched luxuriously in the first bed he'd been in for months. He looked out the window at the lighted patterns of the city. He opened the window a crack, and sounds came in, muffled by distance. It was good

179

to be home. Then he thought of the cabin, the utter stillness of the forest broken only by old Lonesome's forlorn cry, an owl's hollow calls, or a limb scraping softly across a log.

Tomorrow there'd be things to do, some decisions he'd have to face. Thinking of these, he was dragged downward into sleep.

He saw the story in the paper next morning. There was a picture of the three of them all wrapped up in each other's arms. The headline said, GRAYSON'S SON FOUND ALIVE.

After breakfast, Peter made a tour of the house and yard, but he couldn't get the thoughts of Omar, Senator Kaufman, and the tragedy that hung over Omar's Wilderness out of his mind. When he came in, Clara Grayson asked, "Well, got your feet on the ground this morning?"

"A little, I guess."

"Done any thinking about school?"

"Not much. Have you?"

"Some." She folded her arms and leaned against the kitchen table. "Didn't sleep as well as I'd hoped I would last night, so I did some thinking. Excitement wouldn't let go, I guess. Your father slept like a log."

"He would." Peter smiled.

"Spring term's more than half over," she went on. "You wouldn't gain a thing starting this late. You might as well wait until fall, unless you really want to go."

"That's fine with me," he agreed.

She followed him through the dining room. "Is something bothering you?"

"What do you mean?"

"I have the feeling that you're here, and you're not here."

"I guess I'm not quite home yet, Mom. Things have been happening pretty fast the last couple days."

"For us, too," she smiled. "I can't quite believe you're back yet. Maybe it'll take another day."

"I guess so." Peter climbed the stairs and flopped on his stomach on the bed and stared down at the city. He was bothered plenty. He could feel himself being pushed toward a decision he didn't want to make—that he actually feared. It was like being sucked into the current of the canyon, and it was almost as frightening.

He thought about it and argued with himself all day. It's over, he told himself. It was a bad six-month dream. But it hadn't all been bad. Most of it had been a wonderful experience. There had been Omar—old, lean, and tough—wonderful Omar. He was aware his mother was watching him. Several times she was at the point of saying something.

Finally he remembered that last night with Omar—as if he could ever forget it. He could hear Omar's tired voice say, "Man should always fight for what he believes in. Then if you lose, you've got nothin' to be ashamed of. You got to try."

He knew exactly what he was going to do now. Omar had made the decision for him.

That night, Peter waited until they'd finished dessert. "I've been thinking about that hearing in Washington about logging Omar's Wilderness. Senator Kaufman would have liked Omar to testify because he'd lived there so long and knew about the country and the forest. I could go and tell them all the things Omar told me."

George Grayson laid down his spoon. "You mean, appear before that senate committee?"

"Yes."

"Not a chance. You're just a boy, and you'd be up against some of the sharpest brains in the country. Those senators would crucify you."

"I'd only tell the truth. What I know."

"You'd be amazed how the truth can be twisted. You'd be completely out of your depth."

Clara Grayson said quietly, "So that's what's been bugging you all day. I think it's a fine idea. You should go."

"Are you out of your mind?" George Grayson demanded.

"Truth is truth," she said quietly. "It can be twisted, but it's still the truth. You stick to your guns, Peter."

"You sound like Omar," Peter said, smiling.

"He's fifteen." His father's half-angry voice was directed at Peter's mother. "I don't want Pete humiliated and disillusioned."

"He won't be. You said he was just a boy and couldn't possibly survive more than a couple of weeks when he was lost."

182

"I was looking at the facts."

"You didn't have your facts straight then, and you haven't now."

Peter looked at his mother, calm, quiet, smiling, even while his father's anger beat against her. For the first time he realized how amazingly strong she was.

"I know Peter will do all right in Washington," she said. "Just as I always knew he was alive. Peter owes this to Omar. That noble old man meant to fight as best he could to save his forest, the animals and birds and streams he loved. Now Peter should do the fighting for him. It's the only way Peter can pay back the biggest debt he'll ever acquire."

"I don't want Pete hurt."

"Neither do I. But he won't be. Can't you see this is not the same fifteen-year-old boy who took off for the ranch six months ago?"

George Grayson frowned. "It's hard for me to accept that fact completely." He smiled at Peter. "Did you know that your mother can be as stubborn as a mule? Okay, so I'm outvoted."

"Have you thought about what you'll say?" Clara Grayson asked.

"I'll tell them what I told Senator Kaufman. The things Omar told me and taught me. I wish I could show that committee the forest and game and streams in contrast to the Flat Iron Creek area. Then they could compare."

"Maybe you can describe it," George Grayson suggested.

"I will." Peter looked at his father. "Will you pay my way to Washington, Dad?"

"I think Grayson Electronics is good for it. Just one thing, your mother and I are going along as your cheering section. We didn't find you just to lose you again. Okay?"

"I'd like that."

Clara Grayson shook her head. "Declare me out. I couldn't sit and listen while Peter testifies."

"You took the past six months like a trooper," George Grayson reminded her. "We can make it a sort of vacation, too."

"It's different from the search and waiting. Anyway, I think the men of the family should handle this."

"All right. I'll take care of everything, Pete. You don't have to worry about a thing except your speech."

The days passed swiftly. Omar's poke assayed at $2,725, which went into a special account. George Grayson brought home books, pamphlets, and copies of speeches. He helped Peter assemble his notes and facts and weld them into a speech.

Clara Grayson said, "You're more nervous about this hearing than Peter is. Who's making this speech anyway?"

"Those people want facts. Cold, hard facts. I want Pete to do a good job when he gets up there."

"He will," she said.

"You just bet he will."

The speech was written. Peter studied it until he knew it by heart.

184

He practiced on his parents.

"It's good," Clara Grayson said, "full of vital facts and figures."

"These figures'll make 'em sit up and take notice," George Grayson predicted.

"Is that the kind of speech you planned?" she asked Peter.

"Gee, Mom, I don't know," Peter said. "It's not what Omar would say. But Dad knows more about what they want to hear than I do."

The night before they left for Washington, George Grayson came home with twenty-five neatly bound blue notebooks. "You're required to have at least this many copies for senators and others to refer to while you're talking," he explained.

The first two pages were Peter's typed speech. Then there were pages of blown-up photographs. There was Omar's cabin just as he'd left it. There were shots of the river, of the timber stand marching up and up to vanish over the horizon. There was a close-up showing the ground cover and the network of roots. The notebooks contained pictures of deer, elk, and bears. Another picture was of a golden eagle, wings set, soaring over the forest. One picture showed the graves of Omar and Edward Dennis. Opposite each shot of the timber stand or an animal was a contrasting picture of the devastation at Flat Iron Creek. The notebooks even contained pictures of the bone-dry rock bed that had once been Flat Iron Creek and a panoramic shot of the network of log-truck roads and skid roads.

"Where did you get these?" Peter asked. "They're wonderful!"

"I sent a cameraman up there in a helicopter," George Grayson said, smiling. "You know what they say, one picture's worth a thousand words. I figured they'd come in handy."

"They sure will," Peter said. "Senator Kaufman will like these. Thanks a lot."

"We've got to win this thing," his father said. "No two ways about it."

Clara Grayson went to the plane with them the next morning. "Remember," she told Peter, "those committee members are people first and senators afterward. Everything will be fine." She kissed them both, then went up to the observation deck to watch their plane take off.

It was dark when they swept low over the Potomac, the Lincoln Memorial, the Washington Monument, and landed at Dulles Airport.

Peter was too keyed up to eat a good dinner or to sleep. His father kept turning and tossing in the next bed. Finally Peter said, "Can't you sleep either?"

"I always fight a strange bed the first night," George Grayson grumbled.

Peter said, "I'm glad you came. I couldn't go through with this alone."

George Grayson got out of his bed and sat on the edge of Peter's. "Little nervous?"

"Scared," Peter said.

"Good. When you're a little afraid of your audience, it's a sign you'll do well. The prof I took a course in public speaking from told me that. The old adrenalin begins to pump, and every nerve stands on tiptoe. I was just wondering, what do you suppose Omar'd be doing if he was here?"

Peter thought about the lean, tough old man. "He'd

likely get a good night's sleep. In the morning he'd be anxious to get before those senators to tell them what he knew. Happy for the chance to fight for what he loved."

"So will you," his father said. "You've got the facts you need in those folders, and pictures that tell the story. You know your speech. You don't need anything else. Don't worry, you'll do fine, and I'll be right there beside you. Nobody can lick Pete and George Grayson."

Peter felt comforted. His big, solid father was with him. It would be all right.

It was a little after nine when they went down the wide marble hall of the Senate Office Building and turned through the big double doors of the hearing room. They found seats near the back. Peter guessed the room would hold a couple hundred people. It was about half full.

The room was cool. It smelled faintly of floor polish. Up front was the big horseshoe-shaped rostrum where the committee would sit. Directly in front of the rostrum was a long table with microphones for those who would testify. Another table at the left, he learned later, was for the press.

People kept drifting in until the room was nearly full. Some gathered in small clusters and talked. Finally, the big double doors into the marble hall were closed. The door behind the rostrum opened. The committee filed in. Senator Mike Kaufman was in the lead.

He took his place in the center with three senators on either side.

Peter looked closely at each one. Senators Glass and Murphy, Peter guessed, were the oldest. Both wore glasses, and Murphy also wore a hearing aid. He was continually pushing the small button into his ear as if he were afraid it would fall out. Both looked as though they'd been interrupted during a morning nap. Senator Tobin looked to be about Mike Kaufman's age. He was big and sturdy with a deep-lined face. He kept puffing on a cigar. He looked tough and uncompromising. Senator Young was handsome, black-haired. He kept smiling and nodding to members of the press and to others in the audience. Senators Henry and Beck were the youngest. They looked eager and sharp. These were the men he had to convince.

George Grayson leaned down and whispered, "Now keep your eyes and ears open."

Senator Kaufman was cool, businesslike, impersonal. He called group after group. Sometimes there were as many as four people sitting at the table testifying.

James T. Sutton, Jr., was one of the first. He was flanked by three well-dressed men with briefcases. Sutton was an imposing block of a man. His voice held the ring of authority as he spoke of jobs, the number of people employed, the amount of money logging such a tract of timber would bring into the small mill town. His voice sounded grim as he stated, "If we are denied

189

the right to log this stand, our mill will close. This happens to be the last stand near enough to haul to the mill by truck. If the mill closes, the town dies, and literally hundreds of families will be left stranded. The economy of the area will collapse. We don't want that. I don't think you do, either."

The men with him spoke eloquently in his behalf. Afterward, there was a short question and answer session. Senator Tobin puffed intermittently at his cigar, laying it in an ashtray, then picking it up again. He did not seem impressed. Beck and Henry did most of the questioning. Peter thought they seemed impressed by the testimony of Sutton and his assistants.

Others testified singly and in pairs. They all were in favor of logging Omar's virgin forest. They spoke glibly of the great need for lumber for homes and all manner of construction. Of the population explosion and how many million new homes must be built each year. They presented figures on the numbers of people working in the forest industries, how many millions of dollars were contributed to the economy.

When Senator Tobin laid down his cigar, and asked, "Now, what about this clear-cutting business we've been hearing so much about? I think we should go into that some."

They were quick to answer. One after another they pointed out the advantages of clear-cutting as Mountain Home did it. It was cheaper, faster. There were more figures to support the statement. They could put lumber on the market at less cost to the consumer. It was good for the environment. It created jobs and clear spaces where, in sunlight, young trees could grow faster. It increased the browse for deer, elk, and other wildlife. They spoke smoothly, clearly presenting reams of charts and figures to bolster their contentions.

Peter's heart sank. "Facts and figures is what the committee goes by," his father had said. They were being quoted by people who were obviously accomplished and had done this many times before. His father leaned down and whispered, "Those are pros. They're called lobbyists, hired by the timber companies to do just what they're doing."

There were probing questions from the committee, but seldom was there a challenge. Glass looked bored, as though he'd done this a thousand times. Murphy fiddled with his hearing aid. Tobin studied each witness and smoked intermittently. His craggy face said nothing. Mike Kaufman remained cool, impersonal, all business, only now and then speaking a word or two to some witness he knew. Henry and Beck continued to be what George Grayson called "the eager beavers."

Finally, the opposition began to testify. Peter was amazed to hear the same kinds of professional witnesses. Only their testimonies were in definite conflict with those of the lumber interests.

George Grayson smiled at Peter. He whispered, "Pros, too."

The mill town, they stated, was owned by Mountain Home Logging Company. The company expected the town to die when the timber ran out. They'd build another company town wherever Mountain Home went. To harvest this stand would only postpone the inevitable—three, four, or five years. One of the last great stands of virgin timber would be gone, the land ruined forever because of Mountain Home's clear-cutting methods. Clear-cutting was a little cheaper and faster, but the savings would not be passed on to the consumer. It was not good for the environment. Logging roads washed ditches. Water ran off the scalped earth, taking the good soil with it. Streams dried up or became so badly silted that salmon could no longer spawn. Game disappeared. The testimonies went on and on. There were more facts and figures to battle James T. Sutton and his interests. It came to Peter gradually that the facts he'd so carefully marshaled, the statements he planned to make, were being covered again and again. His hands became clammy. There was an emptiness in his stomach. He had no speech. He glanced at his father and saw the sick realization in his eyes. "It's all right," George Grayson murmured. "I'm going up there with you, and you're going to give that speech. It won't be the first time they hear it, but it might be the last."

Noon recess came. There was a lunch break. Everyone returned, and the statements and questions went on and on. It was three o'clock when Peter saw blue notebooks being distributed to the senators. His mouth was dry. He felt a trembling begin in his stomach.

Senator Kaufman said, "We have one more witness, Peter Grayson."

192

Peter rose, and his father rose beside him. He was suddenly embarrassed that before all these people his father should walk to that witness table with him. He shook his head and whispered, "Dad, I want to go alone."

George Grayson nodded. He squeezed his son's arm and sat down.

Peter felt the eyes of the committee, the press, and several hundred spectators and witnesses on him as he made his way to the table. A low murmur of surprise ran through the room at the appearance of a young boy.

Senator Kaufman's bright blue eyes smiled at him. "Pete, it's nice to see you again." He looked up. "I'd like to say something about this young man. Peter Grayson, to my knowledge, is one of the youngest witnesses we've ever had in Washington. But don't be misled by his years. He has had more life-and-death adventures the past six months than most of us experience in a lifetime."

Peter sat stiffly while Senator Kaufman told about the plane wreck, the burial of Frank Eldridge, Omar's death, and how Peter lived alone through the winter until the senator's party found him.

Senator Tobin leaned forward, studying Peter intently, his smoking cigar forgotten. Senator Glass was wide awake. Murphy quit fiddling with his hearing aid. Henry, Beck, and handsome Senator Young were all intent. Here was something different.

"This young boy," Senator Kaufman finished, "lived

in the very stand of timber we're discussing. Omar Pickett lived in the canyon. He told Peter a great deal before he died. I'm sure everyone here will find what Pete has to say is of great interest." He leaned forward then and said directly to Peter in a voice everyone could hear, "Incidentally, Pete, you don't happen to have a chunk of jerky with you?"

Peter had to smile. "No, sir." Something tight in his stomach began to let go.

Senator Tobin cleared his throat. "Did I understand the chairman to say 'Omar Pickett,' the old canyon rat?"

"That is correct, Senator."

Senator Tobin said to Peter, "I met Omar some years ago when I made the trip upriver. I'm sorry he's gone. Burying him was a rough thing for a boy to have to do."

"He was my friend," Peter said.

"Now, Pete," Senator Kaufman said, "I understand you came because you wanted to testify for Omar."

"Yes, sir."

"We'll be glad to listen to anything you care to tell us about the country and the things Omar Pickett told you. Take your time."

Peter cleared his throat. "What I meant to say is in those notebooks. But everybody else has already talked about them."

"Your speech will be entered in the record along with any remarks you make now. So why don't you just go on?"

Peter hesitated. Then he thought of Omar and began, "Omar was born about a hundred miles from the canyon and that stand of timber. I call it Omar's Wilderness because I never heard any other name. When he was young, Omar guided hunting and fishing parties into that country. Finally, he went to live there. He built a cabin, did a little mining, and lived there fifty years. He claimed squatter's rights. He called them his forest and his animals. He was always patching up a deer that got hurt, or a bird, or a coyote, or a bear cub." The tension was gone. Words tumbled out. He had the odd sensation Omar was sitting beside him.

"Omar studied the timber, the land, the animals, and the streams. They were his life." He opened his own blue notebook. "If you'll turn to page three."

On the rostrum seven attentive senators opened seven notebooks. "My father had these pictures taken just a few days ago. That first picture is the cabin Omar built. The next two I call Omar's Wilderness. It is the stand of virgin timber Mountain Home Logging Company wants to log and that others here want declared a wilderness area. Omar said it took a thousand years, maybe more, for that forest to become what it is. Once logged, it will be gone forever. But losing the timber isn't the only loss. If you'll turn to the next page, you'll see some of the wildlife. There are deer, elk, bears."

Peter was turning the pages slowly and every member of the committee was following. "There are a lot of golden eagles. We haven't any pictures of coyotes, bob cats, cougars, or goats. But they all live in that forest. Game is thick. It's so tame that all you have to do is whistle or sing, or make some small noise to alert them that you're coming. They won't bother to run away."

Senator Kaufman glanced up and smiled.

Peter went on: "Once that land is scalped—that's what Omar called clear-logging—the game will disappear."

Peter turned another page. "This is a shot of the forest floor and the ground cover. You can see the network of tiny roots. They hold the land from being washed away during heavy rains and thaws. Huge logging machinery and logging roads will destroy those roots and ground cover. But there is more to lose than game and torn-up land which no longer grows anything. That forest feeds a number of salmon-spawning streams. Many will dry up once the timber is cut. Others will be silted up so bad the fish can't spawn. The salmon run will disappear."

Peter turned another page. The senators followed. "This is Flat Iron Creek today. It was once a big spawning stream, as you can see by the width of the rock bed. Thousands of salmon came up here every year to spawn."

Again he turned a page. "This is the reason Flat Iron Creek went dry. Once this wasteland was a great stand of virgin timber. Mountain Home 'cut-out and got-out' about thirty years ago. They left behind what you see. Mountains of rotting debris, rotting stumps, logs, and torn-up earth that grows only a few weeds. That picture was taken less than a week ago. A new forest hasn't even begun. It can't. There is no topsoil left to feed one. Omar's Wilderness will look like this if it is logged."

Peter's words came faster and faster. Every senator's eyes were glued to his notebook. The only sound in the room was his young voice. And he was hearing again Omar's angry words as he'd described the felling of the tree with the young eagles in it, dragging logs through the stream, and scattering the spawning salmon, the gun-happy hunters who used the game for target practice. He was so wrapped up in what he was saying that for a brief moment he forgot where he was. Omar's scorching words jumped out. "Omar said that most of the people responsible for the Flat Iron Creek slaughter are gone now, but he hoped they'd fry in hell a thousand years." His face reddened. His voice faltered.

None of the committee batted an eye.

Senator Kaufman said quietly, "Go ahead, Pete."

"Omar said this was one of the largest stands of virgin timber left in the state. It will furnish jobs for a few hundred people for three, four, or five years. When the timber is gone, Mountain Home will leave, the jobs will end. But the mess they leave behind will remain, maybe forever."

He'd said more than he meant to. "Omar mined a little more than $2,700 worth of gold dust. He had another $2,000 in the bank. This spring he planned to

197

use it all and hire a lawyer to try to fight to save that land and virgin forest for all of us to enjoy. He had no way of knowing anyone else would be interested. He had no radio, no papers. If he could be here now, he'd be happy to know there are others who care."

Senator Kaufman said, "I believe this ends Mr. Grayson's testimony. Are there any questions? Senator Tobin?"

"Do I understand, young man, that you and, ah, Omar, are opposed to all clear-cutting?"

"No, sir," Peter said. "There are places clear-cutting can be done. But not on the slopes and tops of mountains where water runoff can gouge out the soil."

"How old did you say you were?" Senator Tobin asked.

"Fifteen, sir."

"I'd like to hear you again in another fifteen years," the senator said dryly. "I've no further questions."

Senator Henry said, "You spoke of a thousand years for that forest to grow back. Why a thousand? I've seen forty- and fifty-year-old trees that looked pretty good."

"They must have been in the valleys, on good soil. Hill soil is poor soil. And this stand that I call Omar's Wilderness is in the mountains."

Senator Beck said, "You kept comparing this timber tract to the ravaged Flat Iron Creek. Why?"

"Both have the same kind of soil. Both are in the mountains. Omar said it took as much as three hundred years to build one inch of topsoil on those

198

slopes and mountains. That's why the trees grow so slowly."

Senator Murphy punched at his hearing aid. "You say wildlife will disappear. I understand that clear-cutting gets sunlight on the ground and promotes faster growth of vegetation and makes food for game."

"Yes, sir. In some places," Peter said. "But not all. Flat Iron Creek is one. You see nothing growing in that picture. And what game there is can be easily run down on those logging roads and killed. There's no place for wildlife to hide, to raise their young."

There were more questions. Peter found the answer, either in what Omar had told him or in what he had observed himself. Sometimes he found it by remembering something he'd read in the books, pamphlets, and speeches his father brought him.

Then the questions were over. Senator Kaufman thanked him for coming and asked, "Is there anything else, Pete?"

Peter thought of Omar, and of the great stand of timber marching into the sky. He thought of Solomon and Marty and Bill and all the wild animals who lived in that ancient forest. He thought of the disaster of Flat Iron Creek.

"Yes, sir," he said, "I'd like to say one thing for myself." He drew a deep breath and looked at each senator in turn. "Some day maybe I'll have a family. I'd like to take them up where I spent the winter and show them the great trees and all the wild game, and the river and creek so clean. But if that forest is clear-cut, it will be another wasteland. I'll never go. I'd be ashamed for them to learn how bad their country has become."

A hush came over the room. Senator Tobin picked up his cigar, then put it down. Murphy started to tap his earplug. Seven senators quietly closed their blue notebooks.

Peter and his father walked out into the great marble hall. George Grayson's voice was husky, "Pete, no matter what you do, I'll never be more proud of you than I've been the past hour."

People crowded about, shook Peter's hand, and congratulated him. A reporter clapped him on the back. "Pete, read *The Washington Post* tomorrow. I think you'll like it."

James T. Sutton and his group went hurriedly off down the hall alone.

The people melted away. Senator Kaufman came. He shook George Grayson's hand, then Peter's. "You did a good job, Pete," he said.

"How did we do?" Peter asked anxiously. "Did we save Omar's Wilderness?"

"There's no doubt your side did much better than the timber people. Everyone was aware of that, including Mr. James T. Sutton. Your testimony and those pictures helped a great deal."

"But did we save it?"

The senator's blue eyes smiled at him. "From more than twenty years' experience I'd say 'yes,' you saved it. But it will take a little time to become official."

Peter wanted to shout at the top of his lungs. But all he said there in the great marble hall was a quiet, "Wow!"

"I must warn you," the senator continued seriously, "you've only won a battle, not a war."

"But we did win?"

"You won this time. But the same kind of battle will be fought again and again. The price for saving our national resources, and that includes forests, wildlife, and streams, is eternal vigilance. The weight of that fighting will have to be borne by you young people, because the hardest fights are still ahead. So keep your wits about you."

"Yes, sir," Peter said.

They started down the hall, Peter walking between the two men. "How soon are you leaving for home?" the senator asked.

"First thing in the morning," George Grayson said.

"Then tonight you're having dinner with Mrs. Kaufman and me. She wants to meet Pete. Incidentally, what do you sing?"

"Sing?" George Grayson scowled.

"Bass, baritone, or tenor?"

"A very bad bass, I suppose. Why?"

"He doesn't know?" the senator asked Peter.

"I haven't told him." The weeks of uncertainty were over. Peter felt light as air.

"I guess we'll have to take him up there and show him what we mean," the senator said.

"Let's go soon." Peter wanted to stand beside

Omar's grave and tell him there was nothing to worry about. His wilderness would be here forever.

"If you two are talking about going up to Omar's place, I'm taking a fishing rod," George Grayson said. "They tell me there's trout in there you wouldn't believe."

"Trout!" Peter scoffed, "anybody can catch a trout. Now if you happened to be real lucky, you might hook into a goofang."

"A what?"

"You never heard of a goofang?"

"So what's a goofang?" the senator asked gravely.

"Well," Peter said expansively, "a goofang looks a lot like a trout, only different. He's about the size of a trout, only bigger. And he swims backwards. . . ."